ARIEL'S REDEMPTION

Book 5 in
The Winstons Series

Rowena Dawn

Scarlet Leaf
2021

All characters in this book are fictive, and any resemblance to real persons, living or dead, places or events is coincidental.

No events in this book represent a faithful depiction of the Canadian legal system but are inspired by this one.

Toronto, Canada

IN MY FATHER'S MEMORY

ACKNOWLEDGEMENT

I would like to thank **Owen King** from Quora for his consulting about cars. Thank you, Mr. King.

THE WINSTON FAMILY

Rebecca's children
    Adam (m. Anna)
    Evelyne (deceased)
Adam's children
    Marjorie (Twin, m. Jonathan) – children:
        Matt (35; M. Nora, adopted son - Nat),
        Maggie (29),
        Jay (29; m. Ellen)
    Michael (Twin, m. Amelie) – children:
        Josh (27),
        Lily (27; m. Mark)
    Gabriel (m. Emilie) – children:
        Ariel (33),
        Alex (33),
        Becka (20; m. Bryan; twins: Lea and Sean)

CHAPTER ONE

Ariel stifled a yawn while the pastor kept droning on and on about the promise of marriage. The young woman was bored to tears and hated every moment in there. She looked around to see how the others were faring, expecting to see the dismay on people's faces. However, everyone else seemed to listen, enraptured.

The woman turned her eyes back to the front. Standing in front of the pastor, the two red-haired young people held hands, looking one at the other as if no one else were in the room.

The bride's mother and aunts smiled nostalgically, wiping off tears at the corner of their eyes, and some of the men felt the compulsion to pat their hands in sympathy.

Mark, the groom, gazed at his bride, Lily, with wonder in his eyes. Lily always looked beautiful. Still, the wedding dress had turned her into a princess, and Ariel couldn't stop her jealousy.

Through narrowed eyes, the woman watched her younger cousin getting married. Surrounded by happy or nostalgic faces, anger and frustration boiled in Ariel's blood.

The woman had fisted her hands so tightly that her nails left bloody marks in the middle of her palm. Nevertheless, Ariel couldn't care about that. She had to control the fury and bitterness raging inside her.

The young woman tightened her lips to stop the storm of words threatening to leave her mouth. She understood that others wouldn't have looked with kindness over her tantrum. However, Ariel hardly kept her fury in check. Another of her younger cousins was getting married before her eyes, leaving Ariel behind in the dust, with only two more years left to fulfill her destiny.

Tears started to tease the tips of her eyelashes, and Ariel tried hard not to let them fall. Everyone knew of her failures. Ariel needn't give them any more fodder for gossip.

Ariel was thankful that she had no role in the wedding party this time. Everyone convened to reduce the number of bridesmaids to one after Becka got married, and the young woman couldn't be happier.

Green with envy, Ariel took her eyes off the silhouette of her cousin when the pastor invited the coppery-haired groom to kiss the bride. To see the couple kiss would have been beyond her capacity to bear.

Six years younger than Ariel, Lily had already fulfilled her dreams and desires, gaining everything. The young woman found it difficult to look past that.

With a cringe in her heart, Ariel remembered that three others had done it before her. At that bitter thought, the woman's eyes swept over her younger sister Becka, encircled in the arms of her husband, Bryan.

Bitterness brought flames in her eyes, and the young woman turned toward her other two cousins, Matt and Jay, who held hands with their wives, Nora and Ellen. The two couples stirred her envy as well, and her breath hitched. Ariel fought to control her breathing so that no one around could guess the thoughts going through her mind. She didn't need their pity or their disappointment.

That day had started better than Ariel hoped. The groom had been a no show in the morning, and his absence uplifted her mood. But then, at the last minute, the guy marched inside the living room, where the wedding was supposed to take place, and all her hopes crashed, filling her mouth with bile.

Ariel hated neither Lily nor Becka. In reality, she loved them both. They were family and shared a past together. Still, that morning, the young woman felt only hatred. Ariel disliked how it tasted. Yet, her feelings were out of control, and she couldn't get a grip on them.

Sensing someone's gaze on her, Ariel turned her head and noticed Bryan, watching her with compassion in his eyes. The young woman grimaced.

'You can keep your pity! I don't need it,' Ariel scolded the man in her mind and slashed him with a withering look.

"Lily and Mark look so good together," Marjorie whispered from the chair in front of her. Ariel gritted her teeth with annoyance after she processed the words.

She hated that people had to fawn over the couple. Marriages happened, and they didn't always reach their happy-ever-after.

Still, Ariel had to admit that Lily and Mark did look good together. That was another thorn in her claw.

At the end of the ceremony, Mark kissed his bride to seal the marriage, and cheers filled the room. With a stingy smile, Ariel applauded with the others. The smile didn't reach her eyes, though.

People filed to congratulate the two young people and then broke into groups. Aunt Amelie, Lily's mother, helped by a few others, started arranging the chairs around the living room so that the guests could walk around and mingle.

Ariel did her duty to kiss the bride and the groom, and then she looked for a way out. A rich buffet took the entire side of the room, and the young woman went in that direction to busy herself with filling a plate. She imagined that no one would ask her to share hugs or shake hands if she had hers otherwise occupied.

Ariel filled her plate with some pastries, knowing well that Bryan had contributed them to the feast. The delicacies were worth adding half an hour more to her morning aerobics routine. Moreover, Ariel remembered that she hadn't had the time to eat anything else that morning. She needed the nourishment, or she would not have managed to stay through all the toasts, reminding her of what she would never have.

With the pastries piled on the plate in hand, Ariel turned around and scanned the room to find a place to sit in peace and enjoy her treat. From the corner of her eye, the young woman noticed that Matt was talking to Bryan. Both of them were stealing furtive glances at her. She had a good idea about their conversation, so she groaned inside and headed in the opposite direction.

The young woman discovered an unoccupied armchair in a corner and took a seat with a muffled sigh. She hoped that the kitty-corner loveseat would not entice anyone else, and she would be left to her devices. Ariel didn't feel like making friendly chit-chat right then. If it hadn't been for her mother, the young woman wouldn't even have come there, but Emilie hadn't given her a choice.

The woman had just sat down in the chosen spot when she noticed that Matt and Bryan were headed her way. Uncomfortable with the prospect of talking to them, Ariel brushed her fingers through her hair nervously.

In a rebellious mood, Ariel had had her hair cut for the wedding. She admitted that she had done it in a bout of anger, and somewhat, she regretted her haste. However, Ariel had wanted to steal some of the bride's thunder. She did succeed for about five minutes. The young woman did astonish her family when she appeared at her aunt's house that morning.

No one remembered Ariel without long hair. Even in her childhood photos, she appeared with thick pigtails.

The puzzled look on her brother's face that morning expressed what everyone was thinking. However, Alex, her brother, never minced words, so he was the only one to point out that he thought she had lost her mind.

Ariel felt somewhat strange without the weight of her heavy hair. She had had her haircut only two days before. Still, the impulse of brushing her fingers through it every few minutes had almost become an annoying habit. Nonetheless, the woman needed to reassure herself that she still had some hair left.

The young woman bit into a flaky pastry, and her eyes swept over the guests milling around, trying to avoid meeting the glances of the two men headed her way.

Ariel hoped that they might change direction and choose to talk to someone more inviting. Her face didn't show any trace of a smile, and her indifference was far from welcoming. She preferred her solitude.

The woman noticed that most people gravitated around the newly wedded couple, fighting for their attention. Lily's happy laughter rose over the voices coming from different groups. Ariel scrunched her nose, and involuntarily, her fingers tightened around the pastry she was holding. Sugary white powder fell on her dress, but the woman didn't pay any attention to that.

Ariel knew that she had turned into a curmudgeon. Still, she had no control over her reactions. Ariel hurt, and it was difficult for her to feel any joy for her cousin's happiness. She did not wish that Lily were plagued by misfortunes, but wishing Lily well did not enter her thoughts right then.

"How are you, Ariel?" Bryan's voice insinuated in her musings.

Ariel groaned inside and turned toward his voice. Had she paid more attention, the man wouldn't have caught her unawares, and she could have prepared herself for what was sure to come. But then, she had been oblivious to Bryan's progress towards her by design. The woman had adopted the ostrich's technique when confronted with some danger.

Bryan and Matt towered over Ariel, both slightly leaning forward. The woman looked up to them and sketched a cold smile, the hand with the pastry poised half-distance to her mouth.

"Hey, there, guys," Ariel replied in a far-a-way tone of voice, and her aloof response prompted Bryan's left eyebrow to hike up his forehead. "I'm fine, of course," she continued with a slight smirk, waving the hand with the pastry.

The woman knew what Bryan's arched eyebrow meant, but she didn't have any care for it right then. "What about you? Are you having fun?" she continued, trying to convey the idea that she didn't have any worry in the world for the moment.

Matt measured her with thoughtful eyes and then nodded. "We are, but I'm afraid you don't seem to have any, sweetie," he observed.

"Oh, but I do," Ariel contradicted him. "Excellent pastries, Bryan, as always," she congratulated her brother-in-law, that supercilious smile always firm on her lips. "You've outdone yourself this time," she added and then bit into the piece she was holding in her hand, thinking that they might catch her message and go away.

"I'm glad you like it," Bryan nodded. "However, you seem a little out of sorts, Ariel, and I don't like it. Besides, you've retreated in this corner, all by yourself. It makes one wonder, you know," he decided to point out the obvious.

Ariel blinked a couple of times, showing surprise. As always, Bryan went for the jugular and cornered her.

"Have I?" Ariel wondered, and she turned her head this way, and that way, pretending to observe the surrounding area. "I haven't even realized it. I merely wanted to enjoy some pastries and rest for a while. I had a late night last night, you know," she said, with a small secret smile tucked in the corner of her mouth.

'Yeah, as if! I went to bed at eleven. Even the movie I tried watching on the internet turned out to be too boring,' she recollected with derision but didn't reveal any of her thoughts to the two men.

Ariel hadn't been out at night for over four or five months already. She didn't have any reason to go out and all reasons to avoid any dark places. The woman had the feeling that she was living in a cage most of the time.

Matt watched her thoughtfully and shook his head slightly. Even though he refrained from reading his cousin's mind, he couldn't stop the emotional vibes coming from Ariel.

Matt thought of saying something about that. But then, he changed his mind, sure that the young woman wouldn't like to have her emotions dissected right at that moment.

"I am sure you can relax and rest for a while even if you come and join us there," the man tilted his head towards where his wife, Nora, and Becka sat, talking one to the other.

Ariel shifted her glance toward the two women in time to see that Lily and Mark joined them. Realizing that Nora and Becka were talking to the freshly married couple now, Ariel shook her head.

The young woman didn't feel like sharing someone's happiness right then. She preferred to wallow in her own misery.

"I'm pretty sure that I'm quite fine here for the moment," Ariel turned her eyes away from the group. She smiled thinly to her cousin, and her eyes challenged Matt to contradict her.

The two of them had had their spats over the years, and Matt knew that Ariel was a strong opponent. Her sharp tongue had reduced many to tears along the time. She never gave up until she won.

Matt had never been one of the people that surrendered to Ariel. The man was capable of a lot of patience when he had to argue his point of view. However, Matt didn't feel like getting into a quarrel with Ariel right then. He knew that it wouldn't end too well.

The man wanted nothing more but to enjoy his cousin's wedding day. Matt knew that the party would have a happy ending. After all, Rebecca, his great-grandmother, wasn't there to spoil it. He didn't see why he would allow Ariel to do it.

Matt measured his cousin for a few more long seconds, undecided about whether to point the obvious or not.

"Fine," the man chose to say in the end. "Suit yourself," he added, and with a brisk wave to Bryan, they left her to enjoy her meal alone.

"I usually do just that," Ariel murmured behind them, but Bryan heard her and shook his head with disappointment.

"Maybe it's for the best that she didn't accept your invitation," the man said to Matt under his breath. "She can't control her tongue, and I wouldn't like to see that Lily and Mark had had their big day spoiled with venom."

Still, his words reached Ariel, and the woman pressed her lips together with dismay. However, she knew that the man was right. Ariel never could keep her mouth shut, and she felt the need to shred people with words. That need had become more overwhelming lately, in particular, during the last couple of years.

Nevertheless, Ariel didn't think that her habits gave her brother-in-law any leeway to talk about her that way. His unforgivable words needed some payback.

'Maybe not right now, but soon,' she promised to herself, munching another pastry, even though her anger rose and reached new levels.

The thunders in Ariel's eyes prompted a few eyebrows to rise, and her relatives decided that that wasn't the right moment to approach her. The young woman needed to cool off for a while.

However, after about half an hour, Ariel's mother, Emilie, considered that her daughter had avoided the family enough and resolved to determine her to mingle. The young woman sighed with dismay, but then, she agreed to chat with her relatives for a few minutes.

"I've got a terrible migraine today, mom," Ariel warned her mother. "I almost didn't want to go out of the door in the morning. So I won't be staying too long," she pointed out.

Emilie shook her head in consternation and waved her hand with disappointment, but then, she escorted her daughter to a group of cousins and left her there.

The woman knew her daughter well. She didn't have a chance to make Ariel change her mind. If the young woman wanted to leave, she would and on her own terms.

And Ariel did leave twenty minutes later. She felt like suffocating. Lily's happiness drove her crazy, although Ariel knew that her feelings were irrational. The young woman should have been happy for her cousin, but she couldn't.

CHAPTER TWO

'*You looked nice, babe,*' a metallic voice rasped out of the answering machine. '*You'll make a much more beautiful bride than your cousin. We'll have to make that happen soon, although I hate that you cut your hair. You'll have to learn about some boundaries. Don't worry, though. We'll work on that together. I'll teach you.*'

Wide-eyed, Ariel stared at the answering machine. The message she had just played back might have been subtle, but the menace seeped through the carefully chosen words.

The woman's fingers shook. Although there was no one else there with her in the room, and she didn't need to hide what she felt, Ariel fisted her hands. Her temples ached, and a dull pain throbbed at the back of her head.

The thought of calling the police crossed her mind for a moment, but she chased it away at once. It was pointless. Ariel had tried that in the past, and nothing had happened.

The police told her that what she felt was subjective, and anyway, they didn't have too much to work with to catch the guy leaving those messages. They advised her to calm down and read less through the lines. In other words, she needed to ease the drama.

Ariel turned to the window and stared out in the darkness of the night. Imprisoned in her own home, the woman felt powerless.

For the last few months, she hadn't dared to go out in the evening. Once she got home from work, she would lock every door and window, pull the drapes, and hide in the den, too scared of what might have lurked in the dark.

As a rule, the young woman didn't have a very active social life. But now, terrified because of an invisible man, who threatened her freedom and life, she started turning down every invitation she got and became a hermit.

Ariel had given up going out for a coffee with friends or a drink with someone after work. The young woman had the feeling she'd been locked in a cage, where she turned in circles, and she didn't have any chance to escape.

When the phone rang again, she let it go to the answering-machine once more, happy that, at least, the guy didn't have the number to her mobile phone.

The woman decided to cancel the contract for her landline in the morning and went to bed, although she felt restless and knew she wouldn't fall asleep too soon.

That was the cherry on top after having to attend yet another wedding for one of her cousins. Ariel knew that the time passed her by, and she would soon be too old to fulfill her destiny. She hoped that at least she would get the money.

***

The morning greeted Ariel with a grey sky. Heavy clouds warned of snowfalls, and the young woman groaned in dismay. Ariel had lived in Toronto her entire life and learned to drive in winter, but still, that didn't mean that she had to like it.

That day, she had to visit two locations of the nursery she was working for, and she didn't feel like driving. However, taking public transport didn't seem too appealing, either. That early in the morning, the subway was bound to be packed. Ariel had suffered from claustrophobia since a tender age, so she loathed being stuck in closed spaces with too many people.

The young woman went through her morning routine as fast as she could to get on the road ahead of the other commuters. When she got downstairs, the red light of the answering machine blinked, catching her attention, and unnerved, she scrunched her nose.

On tiptoe, Ariel approached the stand where she had installed her landline. She behaved as if someone had been there with her in the house and could have surprised her.

The young woman glanced at the display of the answering machine. The number of messages shocked her and took her breath away. She gasped for a few instants, fighting for air.

When she could draw air into her lungs again, Ariel congratulated herself for turning off that phone the night before. She knew that her family and the few friends she had could get in touch with her on her mobile phone.

The sheer number of messages strengthened her decision to cancel the landline that very day, and Ariel promised herself that she would do it during her lunch break. It was high time to get rid of the psycho that marred her days with those scary messages left on her answering machine.

The accurate information imparted in some of the messages strengthened her opinion that the guy was stalking her. Ariel wasn't sure, but he knew too much about her personal and professional life. It stood to reason that the man followed her around, although the police were not sure that that was the case. One of the officers had even asked her if she might have exaggerated when Ariel contacted them the first time.

The woman listened to the beginning of the first few messages and turned white. The tin voice gave a detailed account of her moves around the house before going to bed.

Despite what the police said, that guy did represent a menace to her. She needed to solve that situation, and once and for all.

Ariel put on a red, short winter coat and brushed her fingers through her blond, straight locks nervously. She threw a quick glance at her reflection in the mirror without taking note of anything. Then, the young woman gathered her things and started to the front door.

Once more, the anxiety had brought throbbing in her temples and fluttering in her chest. Ariel knew she wasn't in any way fit to drive, but she didn't have another choice right then. After hearing her stalker's words on the tape, the woman didn't dare to call a cab. She couldn't know who would turn up at her door, and it wasn't worth it taking stupid risks.

Ariel hesitated to go out and stopped in the doorway. Her careful eyes scanned the street, but the woman didn't see anything out of the ordinary. She didn't notice any unknown cars parked in the driveways. No people were walking around without a specific purpose.

The woman gathered her courage and went out of the door, pulling the heavy oak door behind her with more force than necessary. Her fingers shook on the key when she locked the door, but Ariel persevered and turned the key in the lock twice.

With quick steps, Ariel climbed down the flight of stairs to turn into her driveway. Her boot caught a patch of ice, and the woman practically fell to the ground.

Ariel yelped but managed to keep her balance, waving her arms in the air like a drunken stork. The rate of her heartbeat went up, and the woman exhaled with a whoosh.

Once she became steady again, Ariel trudged toward her car on shaky legs. The woman pursed her lips and shook her head in consternation. She wondered how it was possible to have ice right at the bottom of the steps.

Ariel had paid her neighbor's teenage son to clean the snow off her stairs and driveway two days before. She knew that it hadn't snowed or rained since then.

Nonetheless, the woman had too many things on her mind right then to ponder on that strange occurrence, and with another shake of her head, she let it go.

CHAPTER THREE

In winter, the light of the day has already faded at four o'clock in the afternoon in Ontario. The gloom of the sky oppresses practically everybody, and moods start changing.

'No wonder the depression skyrockets during the winter months,' Ariel mumbled, carefully climbing down the flight of stairs to the street, dissatisfied with the sudden obscure.

Ariel loved the sun and the light of the day, even if it was filtered through tree leaves or curtains hanging at windows. Winter didn't hold any charm for her. It usually meant a bout of flu, sliding on the pavement, and wearing heavy clothes.

At the bottom of the steps, the woman also took care to throw a long glance along the street, verifying every shadow in sight. Her eyes swept every bush and cranny carefully.

The last events had frightened her. Finding herself in the empty street at that time of the day wasn't something Ariel liked. Her heart started beating fast, and her pulse went up.

Not an hour earlier, Ariel had received a new message from her stalker, and this time on her mobile phone. As she had already canceled the landline in the morning, the woman had hoped that the creepy messages would stop. She didn't seem to have any luck in that area, though.

That new message shocked Ariel and froze her to the bones. The young woman hadn't thought that her stalker could find her mobile phone number, which wasn't even listed. The idea that he had succeeded in putting his hand on it terrified her. She didn't know how she could protect herself from someone with such abilities.

To make the matter worse, the young woman hadn't noticed that the voicemail came from a hidden number, and she listened to it. The words still resonated in her mind, although she had tried hard to push them aside.

Now, she was sure that the guy followed her around, so Ariel surveyed her surroundings with careful eyes once more. She expected that someone would jump out from behind the decorative bushes lining the driveways.

Ariel felt her heart in her throat. Still, the woman continued to make her way toward the spot where she had parked her car earlier. Ariel needed to get to her car and get away from there fast. She didn't have anyone to help her out there, and the man had to be around somewhere.

'How else would he have known that I wear a short red skirt and coat?' Ariel wondered, her eyes darting this way and that way.

That metallic voice from the voicemail had scolded her for wearing slutty clothes and promised to teach her not to show the goods to anyone else but him.

The viciousness of that voice had frozen her for a few moments. The woman knew that she was alone in the office, and only one old guy guarded the premises. That thought scared Ariel even more.

When the phone rang again, she had simply rejected the call. She didn't need to hear that voice and didn't intend to listen to any more voicemails.

Ariel fumbled with the reports in her haste to finish faster and leave that place as soon as possible. Her need to get to a spot packed with people urged the woman to hurry in her work even more. She was convinced that no one would dare to attack her there.

Nevertheless, her lack of attention to the task at hand made Ariel spend half an hour more in the building. She swore viciously for the entire time and cursed her inability to put everything aside so that she could finish sooner.

Ariel marched toward her car with determination, all the time searching warily every driveway and every dark spot with her eyes. The moment she reached her red Mini Cooper, Ariel breathed a sigh of relief, knowing that she would be safe in her car. She would hide inside, and no one could reach her in there. The locks on the doors worked just fine.

The very next second, the note under the windshield wiper caught her gaze, and her breath hitched. Her eyebrows hiked up her forehead, and terrified, the woman took a step back.

Her eyes swept over the automobile to see if anyone had dented it. As she didn't notice any sign that someone had bumped into her car, Ariel's pulse went up a notch. Something didn't seem right.

With shaky fingers, the woman snatched the note from under the windshield wiper. After searching the street with careful eyes once more, Ariel read it.

'The time is close. I can't wait, babe. I'm sure you can't wait, either. See you soon.' An X at the bottom of the page attracted the woman's gaze, and she felt nauseated.

Ariel gasped and then threw another fearful look around. Her fingers balled the paper for a moment, but her logical side reared its head and advised her not to shred it to pieces.

The woman would have liked that. It might have been a small gesture, but at least Ariel might have felt in control over something.

Still, reason told Ariel that she might need that paper later. That note would have proved to the police that she hadn't invented things, and someone stalked her. Those snarky officers couldn't refute such tangible proof.

Now, concerned, Ariel hurried to the driver's side and unlocked the car's door. She got into her seat and threw her laptop case and her handbag on the other one. At the same time, she locked all the doors.

The woman shoved the key into ignition swiftly, turning it. Then, she pushed the lever into first gear, at the same time, stepping onto the clutch transmission. No familiar sound shredded the silence, and Ariel grimaced with dismay.

Something didn't seem right. Ariel eased the clutch a bit and tried again. No sound came from under the hood, and the woman cursed like a sailor, thumping her hand on the steering wheel.

Ariel understood the underlying message. She didn't buy into the absurd idea that her car simply broke while she spent time in the office. Someone must have done something to it.

Ariel didn't need that right then when she had to leave that place as soon as possible. The woman knew that the maniac might have still been around, and the old guard from the office didn't look fit to fight a younger attacker or any kind of attacker.

With an exasperated groan, the woman snatched her belongings from the other seat and climbed out of the car. She headed with quick steps back toward the building entrance when a shadow suddenly came in her peripheral vision and prompted her to run.

Ariel forgot about residual snow or patches of ice on the pavement. Her eyes remained glued on the building entrance, and all her thoughts mingled in a mantra call for safety. Her heart beat in her chest loud, and the sound resonated in her ears.

The woman ran up the stairs and pushed the door open. Pumped up, Ariel didn't stop to catch her breath until she had reached the illusory safety of the lobby.

"Oh, Miss, have you come back already?" the guard wondered from behind the front desk. A moment later, his eyes widened when he noticed that the young woman appeared to be out of breath.

Ariel couldn't speak, so she nodded, trying to pull air into her lungs. She sounded like a seal -- puffing and groaning. The problem wasn't the distance she had run. She got winded because of the exertion coupled with fear.

"I have a problem with my car," the woman managed to utter after a few moments. "I will need to have it towed and fixed," she added grimly, taking her phone out of her bag to call the road service.

If the guard wondered why Ariel had to come back into the building to call CAA for emergency road service when she could call them from her phone, he didn't say anything.

The man contented himself to watch the woman pacing and then answering various questions coming from the other end of the line. However, the woman spoke very low, and the old man couldn't make sense of her words.

"I'll wait for them here," Ariel turned to the man at the front desk when she ended her conversation. It cost her some effort, but the woman spoke in a confident tone of voice so that the man wouldn't contradict her. "I will see their lights when they come," she explained, and the guard nodded.

The man presumed that Ariel was cold outside, and that was why she preferred to wait inside the building. Anyway, he didn't mind her presence.

Besides, he didn't think that the clothes the woman wore would have been appropriate for spending too much time outside in that freezing atmosphere. She would have turned into an icicle in a few minutes.

Admiring the young woman's silhouette, the guard admitted to himself that she would make a tall, beautiful icicle, but he decided against voicing his thoughts. He didn't think that the woman would appreciate his evaluation.

Ariel chose a spot from where she could survey the outside. She kept an eye out not only for the CAA truck but also for the possible stalker. The woman knew that her car had worked just fine earlier. That it broke suddenly now seemed quite suspicious.

The young woman bit her lower lip, rubbing her hands anxiously. The police had made it clear that they didn't buy into her suspicions. She couldn't look for assistance in that direction. It was high time she had found someone else to help her.

Ariel keyed the pin on the screen of her mobile phone to unlock it. Then, she thought of dialing her brother's number. Alex had remained her closest friend, even though they had had lots of disagreements over the years.

They didn't share too many physical traits, although they were fraternal twins. However, they did share the same selfish outlook in life. Consequently, they often came to blows because none of them wanted to concede something.

Ariel fast dialed the number and waited for her brother to answer her call.

"Hey, there, Alex," she greeted him. She had wanted to sound less concerned, but tension seeped into her voice.

"What now, Ariel?" Alex replied, and the callousness of his crisp words slashed through Ariel, rendering her silent for a few moments. "I don't have time for anything right now. I'm in the middle of something. Call me back later," the man hurried to say and disconnected the call without waiting for her answer.

For a couple of seconds, Ariel stared at the phone in her hand with wide eyes. She couldn't believe that her brother didn't even bother to hear what she had to say.

The woman knew Alex and his impression that he was the center of the universe. Still, she expected him to show her some consideration and fraternal concern.

Ariel bared her teeth, but she controlled herself and didn't give in to the impulse to shout in frustration. The old guard might have had a heart attack, and she had enough on her plate to deal with right then. She didn't need any more grievances.

The woman breathed deeply to let the tension seep out of her body. When she considered that she had calmed enough, Ariel dialed Bryan's phone number. The voicemail kicked in immediately, and she frowned.

'What the heck? No one's available anymore?' she wondered with exasperation.

Ariel decided to call Bryan at home, hoping that the man had left his mobile phone somewhere in the house and didn't hear it. The young woman let the phone ring about ten times, but then she had to admit that no one was home, which seemed strange. Becka might have been at the university, but at least the housekeeper should have answered the phone.

'Maybe the children are at their grandparents',' the woman thought. *'They must have given the housekeeper the day off,'* Ariel concluded after a few seconds. *'What now?'* she pondered, knowing that Matt and Jay had plans to go to Montreal with their wives that day and couldn't help her.

Then Ariel remembered that she had saved the phone number for the Jodo that Bryan owned, and she dialed it immediately. The phone rang three times, and a feeling of defeat overwhelmed her. No one would answer her call that evening.

When a grave voice reached her ears, she couldn't stop the feeling of relief and dismay at the same time. *'Of course, Max had to answer my call today,'* Ariel grimaced.

She remembered well Bryan's business partner and friend, the man who would bother her every time their paths crossed, and he laid eyes on her. The thought that Max might have been her only chance to leave that building in one piece that evening made her grit her teeth.

Max repeated his greeting, and his voice betrayed his confusion. The man didn't understand why someone would call the dojo and not speak when their call got answered.

"Hello, Max," Ariel said after a few seconds. "It's me, Ariel," she introduced herself, only to hear the low laughter rumbling through the man's chest.

"I'd recognize this voice anytime, Ariel. You don't need to introduce yourself," the man assured her.

"Good to know," the woman replied, and her upper lip curled up with displeasure.

Ariel would have preferred that Max disappeared entirely from her life, but she had to talk to him at that moment if she wanted to get some help.

"Maybe not so good," the man retorted thoughtfully. "Anyways, what can I do for you?"

"Is Bryan there?" Ariel asked, and her heart sank in her boots, afraid that she might not have the luck to find Bryan that afternoon.

"I'm afraid not," Max replied apologetically. "He took Becka to Niagara Falls for the week. She had finished her exams, and Bryan thought to offer her a relaxing break for a few days," the man explained.

"Oh," Ariel exclaimed at a loss of words. She didn't know what to do now. The woman had put all her hopes in Bryan. She didn't know who else to ask for help that afternoon.

"Maybe I can help you," Max tried to assure her, sensing that something wasn't right with the woman. The man knew her voice well, and that didn't sound like Ariel he knew.

"I don't know if you can," Ariel said, and hesitation trailed her words.

The young woman didn't want to owe Max anything. However, the thought of going out of that building by herself again terrified her. The light had almost faded out, and she didn't know what lurked in the shadows. To sleep in the office over the night wouldn't have been a good idea, either. The building didn't offer too much safety.

"You won't owe me a thing," Max reassured her in a confident but soothing voice.

The man had spent enough time trying to read that woman and understand what made her tick. So, now, he was able to guess her thoughts with some accuracy.

"Don't forget that if you need anything, I'm here for you," Max stated with confidence.

Ariel didn't say anything for a few moments, and the man started losing his patience. Max had been chasing that woman for far too long, and the thought that he had wasted so much time upset him.

The man knew well that she didn't care for his presence. Ariel had proved it every single time they ran one into the other. It was high time he had stopped behaving like a stupid teen and asserted his self-confidence.

"Look here, Ariel. If you need help, I'm here for you. Now, if you don't have anything else to say, I'm going back to work," Max said, satisfied to notice that his voice didn't betray his annoyance with himself and her.

"No, no," Ariel rushed to speak at once, afraid that the man would disconnect the call.

Max seemed to be her only hope for that night, and she didn't want to lose it. She might have preferred to avoid him, but she couldn't afford it right then.

"My car broke, and I do need help if you have the time to come and assist me," she added, remembering the words Alex had told her earlier. Ariel didn't believe she would forget them too soon. The woman hadn't thought that she meant so little to her brother.

"Yes, I can come and take you," the man assured Ariel, understanding what she needed. "I assume that you have already called CAA," Max asked her with concern in his voice.

The man didn't like the thought that the young woman was alone in the street in a broken car. The light of the day had already disappeared, and he didn't think that a woman would be safe in Toronto at night, even though rarely something happened in the city.

"Yes, and I think I can see their truck now," Ariel replied after looking out of the window. The headlights sweeping the street had attracted her attention.

"Good," Max approved. "Give me the address where you want me to come, and I will be there as soon as possible."

Ariel took the phone from her ear and threw a long, befuddled look at it. The woman couldn't believe that Max would leave everything at once to come to get her when her brother hadn't even bothered to listen to her.

"Ariel, are you still there?" the man's impatient voice came through the line.

"Oh, yes, of course," the woman answered immediately. "Here's the place where I am," she dictated the address to him. "It's one of my company's locations," she explained.

"All right, give me about fifteen or twenty minutes to get there," Max warned Ariel. "Stay somewhere inside," he added and disconnected the call.

Ariel grimaced again and shoved the phone back into her bag. She knew that she had made her bed that evening, and now she had to play the game.

Still, the man's last words bothered her.

'As if I had humiliated myself by calling him only to stroll outside in the dark like a stupid diva,' the woman mused. She remembered some of the bad horror movies she had seen.

CHAPTER FOUR

"I'm going out to the CAA truck," Ariel turned her gaze to the guard. "Would you mind coming out on the stairs at least? It's dark, and I don't feel very safe," she explained, feeling stupid for uttering those words.

An independent woman always took care of herself, after all. However, that evening, Ariel didn't feel too sure of herself and doubted every move she made.

The man looked at her with some confusion, but then he nodded hesitantly. Women turned out to be fancy creatures sometimes. However, the man had learned not to contradict them too often. That made for a comfortable living.

The guardian knew well the woman he had before his eyes. He saw her every day, after all. She was always dressed nicely. The young woman walked with her head high and looked at people haughtily.

The man had noticed that Ariel liked to play the role of an independent woman. She didn't seem to need anyone or anything to succeed.

To see her asking for help because of the dark seemed a bit of a stretch. The old man had never seen that woman behaving like that. Usually, she would exude confidence and her voice would sound strong, even demanding. Hesitance was not something he would have associated with her.

The old guardian stood up with some difficulty. His joints acted up in winter, and whenever he sat down for too long, he would turn stiff, and the pain became a bit too much for him.

A creak in the man's knees made Ariel flinch. Feeling bad for making the man move, she turned around and rushed out to speak to the driver of the tow-truck. The woman didn't forget to scan the street, frightened that someone would jump her from behind bushes, and she felt relieved when the driver of the road assistance truck greeted her.

The man insisted on checking the level of gas and oil first, and that angered Ariel. She knew that he thought that she was an air-headed woman, and she had just forgotten to fuel the car. The mechanic noticed then that the gas level was way over half, so he thought of popping up the hood.

Once he looked under the hood, the mechanic whistled and then turned back to Ariel. "Now, that's interesting," he noted.

"What's interesting?" she asked him, trying to look into the car over his shoulder.

"Someone cut your sparkplugs wires here," the mechanic showed to her.

At his words, a glacial calm enveloped Ariel. The young woman knew that she needed to ask what the man was talking about, but her throat didn't cooperate. Any words she would have wanted to voice remained locked inside her mind. Anyway, it didn't matter too much. She understood well what the man implied.

Ariel flexed her fingers to control her terror. She stared at the mechanic without blinking, even though her brain had already processed the meaning of his words. Still, the woman tried not to let them touch her, terrified that she would crumble to the pavement and cry hysterically.

"It's interesting that someone cut those wires. Didn't you set the alarm?" the man asked Ariel, tilting his head inquiringly to the right, analyzing the statue-like appearance of her face. Her skin had already turned a marble white.

The woman didn't seem an air-headed creature, and the mechanic had a hard time believing that she would be the kind to forget about setting the car alarm. If not else, she would check at least twice, if not three times, that the warning device worked properly.

As she couldn't speak, Ariel didn't reply for a few seconds but kept her eyes steady on him. She needed time to wrap her mind around his question. The implications alarmed her even more than the cutting of the wires did.

"I did set the alarm," the young woman contradicted the mechanic in a flat tone of voice. "I also remember very well that when I got here to the car, I had to unlock the doors and disarm the device. That means that the system was on at that time," she informed him.

The man searched her face for signs of life. Any color had already left her skin, and Ariel barely moved her lips while answering his questions. The mechanic was afraid that she would faint on him. He didn't do very well with women that turned into a puddle at his feet.

"I understand," the man nodded. The mechanic felt like patting her head to comfort her. However, he knew that such a gesture would have been highly inappropriate. It might even lead to a new seminary about sensitivity and sexual harassment, if not future dismissal with cause. He already had a couple of warnings in his file and didn't need any more grievances.

The woman might have reminded him of a lost child for a moment, but he was still a professional that needed to make a living. Starting patting his customers represented the perfect recipe for getting fired.

"If the person who vandalized your car had hacking software on a custom phone, he wouldn't have faced too much of a challenge. It would have taken a few minutes to hack and stop the alarm, and probably only one minute to cut through the wires if he knew his way around a car," the man explained to Ariel.

At the same time, he wondered if the woman would recover enough to understand what needed to be done. For the moment, she merely stared at him without blinking. The man couldn't read any expression on her features.

"I'll need to tow the car to the garage and fix it there if I can find the needed sparkplugs and wires, of course. If not, you might have to wait a bit," the man explained. "I'll have to order them out," he shrugged non-committedly.

Dejected, Ariel nodded. She couldn't do anything more about her Mini Cooper. She gave the man all the information he needed to tow the car.

The mechanic finished writing everything down and started to the back of his truck. Then, she asked with hesitation in her voice, "Do you think you could write a report for the police about all of this?"

The man turned back to her with interest in his eyes. "In fact, I will have to do that. This is a matter that should be investigated by the police," he assured her.

"Thank you," Ariel said, and then she watched him hook the car to his truck and leave with it.

It hurt more than she had thought it would seeing her car towed away, and the woman hardly could control the tears pooling in her eyes.

That red Mini Cooper was her pride. Ariel had saved a few years to buy it, refusing herself many things in the process. She had gone without a second cup of coffee every day, and sometimes, she even had gone without having lunch. For about two years, the young woman hadn't bought any piece of clothing or shoes, and that represented the ultimate sacrifice for her, as she loved clothes and shoes, in particular.

Now, she felt robbed of much more than the use of her car. Her personal life and dreams and desires seemed to be under attack.

Ariel didn't understand how that hacking software worked, but the fact that her stalker was able to by-pass any alarm system if he wanted to do it troubled her a lot. It meant that she wasn't safe anywhere, and Ariel now wondered if she would ever feel safe somewhere else. If the man had the knowledge to disable alarms, Ariel had nowhere to hide.

The young woman had no doubt that no one else but the stalker had rendered her car inoperable. Probably, he had counted on her remaining stranded on that street, a poor prey at his mercy.

The sound of a powerful engine reached her ears, and Ariel turned her eyes toward the noise. The woman's heart fell in her boots when she noticed that the car came between her and the entrance in the company's building where the guard was.

The vehicle slowed down and stopped in front of Ariel. The driver's door opened, and a pair of long, strong legs, clad in denim, emerged.

Max got out of the car with catlike moves under Ariel's wide eyes. Then the man leaned on the hood of the car, his hands in his pockets and his ankles crossed.

"Is everything all right, Ariel?" the man asked, watching her with careful eyes.

His eyes told Max that the woman was in shock, although Ariel tried to look unconcerned. The man couldn't discern any color in her face, and her eyes seemed a bit too bright because of unshed tears.

"Could we talk on the way?" Ariel asked, approaching his car with hurried steps, unconsciously throwing a furtive look over her shoulder.

The young woman wanted to get as far as possible from that place. She had the sensation that someone was watching her, waiting for their chance to make a move, and she didn't feel like challenging fate.

Max looked pretty scary with his height and bulging muscles, but she didn't want to take any risks. In her opinion, a stalker must have been deranged in some way, and a hulk of a man might not deter him in his plans if he was determined enough.

With a mocking bow, Max gestured toward the passenger's door. His heart might have wept seeing the woman in distress, but he knew better than to show any weakness before her. Ariel needed to get angry before getting out of that paralyzing shock. Soothing words and petting her head wouldn't have worked.

Max was not wrong. Ariel narrowed her eyes to slits, and the woman threw him a quivering glance. Her fingers tightened on the belt of her handbag while she marched toward the passenger's door, her boots clanking on the pavement.

The man held his smile in check. His intention wasn't to enrage her. Max only wanted to make her forget about what bothered her for a moment by directing her upset toward him.

However, he hadn't lost his mind. Max knew Ariel very well. After the first two or three encounters, the man had learned that he needed to disconcert her. Otherwise, she would swat him away as if he were a gnat.

CHAPTER FIVE

After the first few minutes, the silence in the car had become too heavy, so Max turned the music on. Soothing jazz filled the interior, and the murmur of music calmed Ariel. Her fingers relaxed gradually, and she spread them over the bag she had laid in her lap.

Max surveyed her moves from the corner of his eye. Earlier, he had noticed her hands balled into fists, and the man congratulated himself for choosing the right music to help her decompress.

The man didn't like what he read into things. Ariel, he knew, left the impression of being a daredevil, and she was never scared. Right now, she looked like a terrified bunny. The woman surveyed the street with hawk eyes and kept looking in the rearview mirror as if she were afraid that someone was following them.

"Would you mind if I ask you why you keep looking in the rearview mirror?" the man asked in a soft tone of voice, stealing a look at his passenger.

Ariel tensed for a couple of seconds, but then she shrugged.

"Come on, Ariel, something is wrong. I can tell, you know," Max insisted. "Besides, you never said where you wanted to go," he commented. "I'm driving blind here."

The woman pursed her lips with annoyance, and her fingers started fidgeting in her lap once more. The sense of comfort the music had offered her earlier suddenly disappeared. Ariel felt like biting the man's head off for his intrusion into her thoughts.

"Where would you like to go?" she inquired, trying to gain some more time. The woman hadn't thought about a destination, but she didn't feel like going home. The solitude she had previously enjoyed didn't seem so desirable now.

However, the young woman knew that she had to explain what had happened, but she was afraid that the man might not believe her. The mistrust, the police had shown to her, still stung. Besides, Ariel wouldn't have liked to be labeled a scary cat.

Max didn't know what to answer for a moment. Her question surprised him more than anything that had happened that afternoon.

In the regular course of events, Ariel would try to get away from him as soon as possible. Her wish to spend time with him was highly uncommon.

"I have no plans," the man shrugged. "What about you?" Max raised an eyebrow, taking his eyes off the road for a couple of seconds to look at her face, half-covered by the light bangs.

"I don't either," Ariel admitted with a shrug. "But I know that I don't want to go home," she replied more forcefully, clenching and unclenching her fists, upset with herself. The woman loathed her insecurity and inability to control her environment.

"All right then," Max said in a light tone of voice. "What are you saying about going to get something to eat?" he asked her, watching her with concealed curiosity.

The man had thought that he had a good idea about what the woman was like, and her behavior befuddled him.

The woman shook her head but didn't say anything. She didn't know what she wanted, so she couldn't express an opinion right then.

Max glanced at the clock on the board and said, "It's almost time for dinner. Aren't you hungry?" he asked Ariel. "I know I am," he continued persuasively, thinking that food would offer some comfort, regardless of what upset the woman.

"A little," Ariel admitted with hesitation in her voice. "But I don't feel like going and having dinner in a restaurant," she insisted, afraid of going into a public place right then. She wanted to be somewhere where her stalker wouldn't observe all her moves.

"All right," Max nodded, sensing her anxiety. "Then, what are you saying if we buy something, maybe at a drive-through or a fast-food take-out place, and eat at my house?" he proposed.

The man didn't expect her to accept his proposition, but he knew that he didn't have anything to lose.

Ariel watched Max with wide eyes now, at a loss of words. She didn't know if it was a good idea to go to the man's house, but it tempted her. Moreover, the woman couldn't think of another place where she would feel under the radar, far from the stalker's surveillance.

"You know you'll be safe with me," Max stated, staring at her with hard eyes for a few seconds. He didn't like the idea that the woman might fear him.

"I know that," Ariel admitted. The man might have been obnoxious at times and bothered her with his persistent attention, but he never pushed too far. Max had some foggy perception of the boundaries, but he did respect them in a way.

The woman never felt in any physical danger when he was with her. Ariel only feared that she might forget about her family and wishes and give in to his unrelenting persistence. The man also looked handsome like sin. His sex-appeal hadn't always helped the woman to keep her resolve.

"So?" Max insisted, raising his brows inquiringly.

"All right," Ariel accepted. "We can buy something from a fast food take out and then go to your house to have dinner," she decided.

"Do you have any preferences?" Max asked her, turning on a street to the right. Now that he knew where they were going, he needed to change direction toward his home.

"Not really," Ariel replied with an indifferent shrug. "Whatever you want to eat is good for me too," she explained.

"Does Popeye's work for you?" Max continued to drive in a relaxed manner, all the while checking his rearview mirror, interested in finding out what Ariel was looking for. His curiosity level had jumped up a notch for the last few minutes.

"Yes, that's fine," the woman replied in the same indifferent tone of voice that started to annoy him. She gave him the impression that she wasn't even there mentally.

"All right then," Max admitted defeat. He knew that he wouldn't get more from her. "Popeye's it is," he accepted and changed direction toward the nearest location.

Considering how the woman answered his questions, Max knew that Ariel wouldn't muster enthusiasm for anything. However, the man also knew that she liked Popeye's. He had seen her devouring half a bucket by herself once, a feat that had astonished him. Her silhouette contradicted the big appetite Ariel displayed.

Through the grapevine, Max had heard that Ariel followed a vigorous morning aerobic routine. Still, in his opinion, that exercising was no match for the way Ariel ate. Consequently, the man had concluded that Ariel had a very active metabolism. That was the only explanation.

Stopping in front of Popeye's, Max invited her to come with him inside so that she could choose what she wanted to have for dinner.

"No, you go in and order whatever you want," Ariel shook her head. "Someone must remain in the car," she continued with determination, even though Max thought that her explanation lacked any logic.

Nonetheless, the woman didn't want to see a second car disabled that day, and she didn't think that the stalker would dare to break the windows to get to her. After all, Max had parked the car on a busy street, and people were milling around in droves.

"All right," Max accepted, watching the woman thoughtfully. "But when I come back, you'll have to tell me what's going on with you," the man stated in a tone that didn't broach any arguments and then left the car, heading toward the restaurant.

Ariel stuck her tongue out behind him, but the woman had to admit that she had to tell Max what was going on. He needed to know what to expect. Besides, the man might have thought that she was crazy if she continued hiding the reality.

'He probably believes that I'm crazy anyway,' she grumbled, remembering that he wouldn't have been the first to do so.

The woman knew from experience that people didn't believe that someone had a stalker when there was little proof to support that allegation. The police had been very clear about it right from the beginning. They had listened to her but looked at her with pity. Remembering their reaction enraged Ariel every time she thought of that.

Waiting for Max, Ariel attempted to order her thoughts so that she could give him a concise summary of what had happened by then. Still, at the same time, her careful eyes never stopped studying the people passing by the car. The woman was determined to discover the creepy person who had marred her existence for the last few months.

The woman had no idea how the guy looked like, and that drove her mad. However, Ariel was convinced that she could recognize a person with an unhealthy interest if anyone displayed something of the kind.

She focused so much on her endeavor that when Max came back and tried to open the car door, a sharp cry flew off her lips. Then, the woman pressed her fist to her mouth so that she stopped screaming, and the man's eyebrows went high on his forehead.

Max looked at her with curiosity and awe for a few seconds, and then he shook his head at a loss of words and opened the car door. The man passed the chicken bucket and the bag with the other things he bought for them to Ariel and then slid into the driver's seat and fastened his safety belt.

"I'm sorry," Ariel mumbled grudgingly without looking at him.

She felt stupid and ashamed for having reacted that way and didn't know what to do to erase the man's impression that she was seriously unhinged.

Max didn't appear to be in a hurry to start the engine even though the silence prolonged. Ariel stole a look at him from the corner of an eye. The man stared at the woman, half-turned toward her, and his long locks covered half of his face. The shadow of his beard sharpened the line of his jaw, and Ariel felt a kind of stirring in her lower abdomen.

In fact, Ariel felt that way every time her eyes fell on Max, and that off-the-chart attraction disturbed her. No other man had stirred such feelings inside her, and she didn't know what to do with them.

The woman did try to avoid Max and his persistent interest in her, but only because she didn't think that a man should flaunt such a thick long mane or dark tattoos on his arms as he did.

The young woman always associated his appearance with the hell angels, in particular, after she had seen Max riding a mean bike. Ariel was happy that the man hadn't come to get her on that bike that day. She must have been lucky that it had snowed earlier, and it was freezing outside now.

The woman had never ridden a bike and had a healthy fear of anything of the kind. She considered that feeling the wind in her hair didn't make up for the possibility of losing limbs or worse.

In the regular course of events, afraid that she would lose track of the reality otherwise, Ariel avoided lying to herself too much. Therefore, Ariel admitted that she was stuck in old-fashioned beliefs. She did like how the man looked, but her conceptions dictated a specific appearance for a man.

In reality, the woman thought that Max looked hot. No other man she had dated could compete with him. However, Ariel didn't believe that she could go out with a man whose hair was longer than hers and who didn't give a fig about certain social conventions.

Max loved to make people frown over his behavior. The man always did what he considered to work for him and didn't care for other people's opinions. Conventions didn't even enter his vocabulary.

"I think you should tell me what's going on, Ariel," Max said quietly after a while.

Ariel had already stopped waiting for Max to speak, and his voice startled her. Her eyes darted toward him, and her right hand flew to her chest as if she wanted to calm down the furious beating of her heart.

"I didn't want to scare you," Max excused himself in the same quiet tone of voice and reached out to her right hand. "I mean, I noticed you were deep in your thoughts, but I didn't imagine that your mind had wandered in a completely different universe," he added. The man glanced at Ariel, and a smile curved the hard line of his lips.

That smile surprised her. Ariel had seldom seen a smile on the man's face, even when he tried to charm her. The woman had often wondered what that said about Max, but she had never taken the trouble to find out.

In her opinion, the man wasn't someone appropriate for her, as her grand-grandmother used to say. Consequently, the young woman didn't see why she would go out of her way to understand what made him tick.

Besides that, Ariel was sick of the behavior that the men who crossed her way displayed. So, she had given up looking for love for a while. The woman contended with going through the motions of a boring life, finding a fleeting moment of joy here and there.

She mourned not having the possibility of fulfilling her destiny, but nothing more. Love had turned out to be a cruel game, and she had never learned to play it correctly.

"Ariel," Max insisted on getting an answer and pulled gently at her hand. The man realized that she had forgotten about him once more and pondered on God knew what.

The young woman shook her head to clear it, and then she looked straight into his dark coffee eyes.

"I'll tell you," Ariel pushed through her tightened teeth. "But not right now," she added with a bit of warning in her voice. "Let's get to your place first, and then I'll tell you everything," she said, turning her head toward the window to shut him out of her view.

'Not that you'd believe me, of course,' the woman mumbled to herself, pulling her hand out of his at the same time.

"Why wouldn't I believe you?" Max asked, and a deep frown appeared between his brows.

Ariel turned her eyes to him, staring at him with astonishment. She didn't think that he would hear her grumbles. However, his frown puzzled her even more.

"We'll see," Ariel shrugged and abandoned the discussion, trying to make herself more comfortable in her seat. The woman had laid the bag with the other things on the floor. However, she still held the bucket on the corner of her car seat.

Max waited for a few moments to see if the woman would add anything else, but then, he realized that Ariel did mean what she had said. She wouldn't tell him anything more until they got to his house.

"All right, we'll talk at home," the man agreed with her in a low tone of voice. Then, reluctantly, he turned the key in the ignition.

'As if you had had a choice,' Ariel smirked for herself, satisfied that at least that time she won the battle. Petty of her, but she could live with that.

CHAPTER SIX

Max stopped the car in front of a forged gate, and leaning over Ariel, he took a remote from his glove compartment. When his forefinger pushed a button, the gate slid quietly to the right, and the man drove his car inside a large yard toward the garage, whose door had already started to slide up.

Impressed with all that high-end technology, Ariel nodded, pursing her lips, and the right corner of Max's mouth turned up in a satisfied smile. He had been trying to astound the woman for a long time, and now he had finally succeeded.

'To think that what I needed was only a stupid remote-controlled gate and garage door,' the man shook his head.

He was not sure what to believe about the woman he had secretly loved for a long time when she let such frivolous things sway her impression of him. Still, Max didn't dwell too much on that thought.

The man already knew Ariel well enough. They had met because of Bryan a few times, and Max had learned that the number of flaws that riddled the young woman would have been enough for two or three other women.

However, despite her shallow attitude sometimes, the man couldn't get Ariel out of his mind. Since the first moment he had laid his eyes on her, Max had lost the fight with his reason.

The young woman's elflike appearance and what Max thought that he could read in her eyes had robbed him of the will of saying no to his unquenchable desire for Ariel.

At times, Max had scolded himself for his own stupidity of pinning for a shallow woman but then had merely shrugged and continued with his pursuit.

Behind them, the gate slid back and locked, always quietly. The light from the streetlamps reflected in the snow, which lined the driveway. It also lit the dark windows of the house, which flanked the garage on the right side.

Max drove his car inside the garage where the overhead lights had turned on the moment the door opened and parked while the garage door came back in place and cut them off the exterior world.

Ariel swept the area with her curious eyes and noticed with satisfaction that the man was neat. Everything seemed to have a place on racks and in bins. His black bike stood at the far end of the garage, and the light shone over its powerful body.

"You don't like clutter," Ariel remarked with befuddlement in her voice.

The young woman had expected something different from him. Once, her great-grandmother, Rebecca, had said that Max reminded her of the hippies in the 70s. Ariel had never forgotten that observation. She associated the man with the disorder and lack of social norms ever since.

Matt shifted his eyes to her, and a bitter smile curved his lips. The man had a good idea about the thoughts going through the woman's mind at that very moment.

It was not the first time that Ariel seemed stumped by something about him. She always expected certain behaviors from him, and whenever he proved her differently, she couldn't believe her eyes or ears.

"No, I don't like clutter," the man responded matter-of-factly, brushing a lock of hair off his face. "Let's go inside," he invited her and got out of the car without waiting for her answer.

Max walked around the hood and opened the passenger's door, reaching out to take the bag off the floor and the bucket next to Ariel. Then, he reached out to the woman to help her get out of the car.

Reluctantly, Ariel put her hand in his, accepting his help. Max closed the car door and guided Ariel toward the side door, leading inside the house.

Ariel stopped suddenly, and Max turned to her, an eyebrow high on his forehead.

"Is there a problem?" the man asked the woman, fully expecting that she would say that it was inappropriate for her to be alone with him in his house.

"I was just wondering," Ariel started with hesitation, at the same time biting her lower lip.

"About what?" the man asked when she didn't continue her thought, and his dark eyes searched the paleness of the woman's face.

"I suppose you have an alarm system both for the entrance gate and at the garage gate," the woman finally said, and the man noticed that her fingers shook slightly.

Max searched her face some more and then said with reassurance in his voice, "Don't worry, Ariel. I do have alarms both at the gate and the garage door."

Ariel avoided the man's gaze and, watching her own hands clenching and unclenching, said, "But people can by-pass the alarms systems, can't they?"

Max tilted his head to look into her eyes. The top of the woman's head barely reached his shoulder, and suddenly, she seemed even smaller. Fear emanated through all her pores, and the man sensed it at once.

"In theory, any alarm system can be beaten," Max agreed in a soothing tone of voice. "But if you know what you're doing and have back up for any device, then there is no danger," he assured her.

"Are you sure?" she whipped her head up so fast that her bangs bounced into the air.

Max noticed the glimmer of hope in her eyes, and his heart quailed. The woman was beyond frightened. Now he knew for sure that something had happened to her.

"I am sure, Ariel," he took one of her hands in his. "I also have enough back up for my alarms so that no one could trip them all. Nothing bad will happen to you under my roof," Max promised to the young woman, squeezing her hand to comfort her.

"All right," she agreed reluctantly and started beside him with hesitant steps.

"We'll go inside and bring all my safety alarms on line," Max promised, and Ariel released a relieved sigh.

CHAPTER SEVEN

Max led Ariel up a short flight of stairs toward the kitchen door, and once inside the room, he put the lights on. Then, the man left the food on the corner kitchen table and invited Ariel to sit on the bench.

"I'll go to take care of that alarm back-up I told you about," Max grinned at Ariel. "Just wait a few moments in here," he shrugged. "If you want, you can start making some coffee or some tea, whatever you want," he pointed to the coffee maker and the kettle on the counter.

"Don't worry about me. I will manage just fine," Ariel said, waving her hand, and an anemic smile upturned the corners of her mouth.

However, Max noticed that her half-smile didn't reach the light of her eyes, and the man sighed mutely. There was no doubt that something was wrong with Ariel that evening, and he couldn't wait to make it right again.

Max had been thinking about Ariel since the first time he laid his eyes on her at Becka's wedding with Bryan, who was his best friend and his partner.

"I'll get back to you in a few minutes," Max reassured the woman, petting her arm, and then he exited the kitchen with purposeful steps. The man wanted to bring everything online as soon as possible. He remembered that Ariel wasn't a fanciful creature and didn't have the habit of shaking fearfully because of a whim. Something real frightened her.

With no expression on her face, Ariel watched Max leave the room. Once the kitchen door closed behind the man, she headed toward the French doors that opened to the back yard. The young woman looked outside, leaning her head on the glass.

A few lamp-posts lit the yard and the expanse of the garden behind that. Astonishment widened her eyes, and her lips opened in a mute o.

That was the first time Ariel had set foot in that house, and she had never given too much thought to it. She knew that the man was presumably well-off, as he was the partner of her brother in law, Bryan, who owned a dojo in downtown Toronto. After all, Bryan didn't do too badly for himself. However, the woman had never expected that Max had so much space for himself.

Ariel looked at the thick trees for a few moments. The woman couldn't see too much of the flowerbeds because of the snow. Still, she noticed that the garden had a geometric design, which impressed her. She loved nothing more than an orderly garden.

Ariel also admired the shapes of the bushes scattered along the alleys.

The horticulturist in her appreciated the work that went into that endeavor. Max must have slaved for hours to grow that garden or must have hired a landscaping company. Either way, someone had done an excellent job there, and Ariel felt jealous that she wasn't the one to have made her vision come to life in that spot. Her trained eye found a few things that could have been tweaked.

That area would have been a landscaper's dream come true. Large enough, its topography made it perfect for experimenting with various ideas. That was her long-time dream, and there was no room for comparison between that garden and what she had behind her house.

Lost in her thoughts, Ariel didn't even notice when Max returned to the kitchen. The man stopped near the eating area and leaned his hip on the side of the table. He tilted his head with curiosity and watched her reflection in the glass of the French doors, wondering what went through her head.

Max had tried to understand that woman for a long time, but he had discovered that that was not an easy feat. He had found out that she had a materialistic side, and he had witnessed it more than once. In the wake of his findings, the man had also often questioned the wisdom of his feelings for Ariel. Max had noticed her shallowness in some matters, and he could not forget that.

Max didn't know if what he felt for that young woman was love or mere lust. The woman's elflike appearance, the green of her eyes, and the lightness of her hair had attracted him at the beginning. The man admitted that.

Still, he sensed that there was more to her than what met the eye. If he dug hard, he could find something else behind her visible superficiality and love for appearances.

That might have been wishful thinking on his part, but he still clung to that because otherwise, it meant that he plainly deluded himself.

'And probably I just like the punishment that comes with my feelings for her,' Max laughed at himself, remembering the way that woman had behaved towards him in the past.

Ariel might have needed his help now, but that didn't mean that he rose in her esteem. The woman hadn't even wanted to call him. She was just looking for Bryan and found him available instead.

The man shook his head to clear his mind. Max knew that he needed all his mental faculties around that woman. Ariel had slashed him to pieces more than once in the past. Afterward, he had promised himself that he wouldn't allow her to do that to him anymore. He needed to grow a backbone and stand up for himself.

"I took care of everything, Ariel," he said in a quiet tone of voice, not to startle her.

Still, a cry flew off her lips, and wide-eyed, Ariel turned to him. Max noticed that all color had vanished from her cheeks and shook his head with dismay once more.

"I am sorry," the man started toward her. "I didn't mean to scare you," he continued in a soothing tone of voice, reaching out to curve his fingers around her elbow and lead her back to the table.

Ariel seemed quite shaken up, and Max didn't want to see her slide to the floor. That wouldn't do for her first time in his house, and if he had it his way, the woman would spend many other days at his place.

The woman managed to get to the bench and sat down carefully, rubbing her chest with shaky fingers.

"I am sorry," Ariel found the courage to raise her gaze up at Max after a few seconds.

Her eyes roved over the expressionless face of the man and then stopped at the darkness of his pupils. The woman couldn't read his thoughts, and she cursed her inability to use her natural gifts. At that moment, Ariel would have given anything to know what the man was thinking.

"No, it was my fault," Max cut the apology exchange short, waving his fingers dismissively.

The man had other things on his mind and considered that they had beaten around the bushes enough.

It was high time Ariel had revealed what was going on with her. She needed to let him know what had put that scared doe-look in her eyes. Max had enough patience in the store, but he had his limits, as well.

It was high time Ariel had revealed what was going on with her. She needed to let him know what had put that scared doe-look in her eyes. Max had enough patience in the store, but he had his limits, as well.

However, Ariel wanted to make things right, and she looked up at Max, searching the man's face. Then she understood that Max didn't try to be polite but merely wanted to end that stupid discussion. It didn't matter to him whose fault it was that Ariel was startled all the time, so the woman changed her mind at once. She contented to nod and fold her hands in her lap, not knowing what she should do next.

"All right, then," Max sighed inaudibly. "I think we'd better eat that chicken now. It will get cold soon," the man gestured toward the chicken bucket on the table. "I suppose I have to give you a real plate and cutlery before we shared the meal," Max added matter-of-factly. Then the man headed toward the cupboard to take the items out and bring them to the table.

In the beginning, Ariel frowned, considering that the man wanted to ridicule her. Then, she thought better and concluded that Max had sounded indifferent enough. That thought helped her to let it go.

Anyway, the young woman did require a plate and cutlery to eat her food. Scared or not, she didn't intend to forget everything about proper table etiquette and turn into a savage.

She didn't care what anyone else thought about that. Ariel held her principles dear, and if anyone didn't like it, they could go and hang themselves.

Max came back with two plates and forks and laid them on the table. He pulled the napkin box closer to them and, with a gesture, invited Ariel to dig in.

"I should wash my hands first," she said haughtily.

"I thought you've already done that while I was taking care of the alarms," Max retorted, and his left brow curved up.

"I don't know where the powder room is in your house," Ariel replied with an indifferent shrug.

"Powder room?" the man inquired, and the shadow of laughter vibrated in his words.

"It's that room, you know, where one can wash their hands, powder their nose..." Ariel started to explain with a frown between her brows, but Max put up his hand to stop her.

"I know what that is," he retorted drily. "I didn't expect to hear that expression out of historical novels. That's all," the man explained in a cold tone of voice. "However, I can show you where the washroom is," Max invited her to stand up, waving his fingers in the direction of the kitchen door.

Ariel stood up, her cheeks powdered with a pale rose. *'Darn, he does look like one of those heroes in the historical novels, even though he is an ass sometimes,'* she thought, glancing at the man's dark long locks and goatee.

At the first sign of butterflies in her belly, the woman glanced at the man's face. When she met the amused expression in his eyes, Ariel immediately darted her eyes to the floor and started toward the door with quick steps.

'Good going, Ariel,' she admonished herself, upset to have let the man glimpse in her thoughts. *'I think I am too shaken to think clearly today,'* she mused, getting out of the kitchen. *'Otherwise, he wouldn't be able to read too much of my thoughts,'* the woman admitted.

Once out of the room and in the living room, Ariel turned inquiringly to Max. She didn't know where to go from there.

"Straight ahead, Ariel," Max gestured to the other side of the living room, lined with three doors.

"Which door?" Ariel turned to him and asked, fed up with everything. "There are three of them."

"I said straight ahead," Max pointed out. "That means the one right in front of you," he patiently explained as if he had talked to a small child.

Annoyed with him, Ariel grimaced, and with quick steps, the woman headed toward that door. Max watched her, and an ironic half-smile flourished on his lips.

"I'll be waiting for you in the kitchen," he called after her and then returned into the room, shaking his head and biting his lower lip not to burst into laughter.

Sometimes Ariel amused him with her perpetual game of lady of the manor. The woman did like to leave the impression that she never could be in the wrong. She considered that no one had a sharper mind than she, and her education and style reached a higher level than those of the mere mortals.

Max disagreed with her self-evaluation, though. He had seen several gauche pas on her side. Still, her attitude never ceased to amuse him.

CHAPTER EIGHT

Max did not press any confessions out of Ariel during their impromptu dinner but decided to let her eat in peace. He knew that the woman wouldn't go anywhere too soon, as she still looked scared.

After all, Bryan was away with his wife and not available to her. Matt and Jay had also left the town that day and wouldn't return for a few days, so Ariel didn't have anyone else to turn to and ask for help.

Max knew her twin brother, Alex, as they had met a few times at Bryan's. Alex had also visited the dojo a couple of times and showed promise. However, the man didn't seem to have the will to pursue anything to the bitter end. He had chickened out of his training after only two classes.

Talking to Alex those few times, Max understood that Alex held his wishes in the highest regard. No one and nothing else mattered.

Max doubted that Ariel would find her name high on that list with vital matters. If Alex had something else in mind, nothing could have swayed him to help his sister.

Ariel and Alex were twins and as close to one another as two self-centered people could be. However, if Ariel had found herself in the situation to ask Max to help her, that meant that Alex either wasn't available or didn't bother to assist her.

In the beginning, Max attempted some small talk, but the woman's brief answers didn't invite to follow-up conversation. After a few tries, the man gave up and contented himself to eat in silence. Nevertheless, his attentive eyes kept sweeping over her face as he tried to guess what might have crossed her mind.

Once they finished the dinner, Max cleaned the table and put the plates into the sink. Leaning on the kitchen counter, he turned to Ariel and watched her for a few long moments.

"Let's go to the living room and talk about what brought you here," he proposed. "Would you like some coffee to go with that or some wine?"

Ariel raised a brow and looked at him as if he had lost his mind.

"I beg your pardon?" she said haughtily.

"I just wondered what you prefer – coffee or wine. You know better than I what would help you to relate the entire story to me," the man pointed out. "You know that you will need to tell me everything if you want me to be able to assist you. Besides, we haven't spent so much time together that I could know your likes and dislikes," he shrugged.

Max was aware that his words were meant to make Ariel remember how she had always gone out of her way to avoid his company.

The man knew that he turned out somewhat petty but considered that he was entitled to react like that. Ariel had never gone out of her way to make him feel welcome when they ran one into the other in the same place.

Ariel pursed her lips and scrunched her nose. She understood what Max meant. The woman had never shown any friendliness towards Max. She knew that. However, she had always had her reasons and didn't think that she should apologize for her behavior.

The young woman didn't think that having an affair with that man deserved losing everything. Max was one of the most handsome men she had ever seen, and he attracted her like no one else. However, she was smarter than that. She had learned the hard way that a man might be there for a moment but gone in a second.

Besides, Rebecca, her great-grandmother, had been present most of the times that Ariel and Max had been thrown together. The older woman had made no mystery of the fact that she loathed Max. Rebecca had decreed that the man belonged on the lowest rungs of the evolutionary scale.

The old woman couldn't stand the man's hairstyle or tattoos. In her book, both showed low class, and she didn't understand to mingle with such people. Rebecca had met Max at Bryan's a few times, and she had tried to ignore him with all her might. Of course, welcoming someone like him in the Winston family didn't even bear consideration for a second.

Ariel might have given up her chance to find love and her happy-ever-after. She might have also grudgingly accepted that she would never reach fulfillment and have her powers as a witch. However, the young woman had never given up the hope that she could convince Rebecca that she was the best choice for the trust money.

After all, most of her cousins and her sister refused to touch that money, and soon enough, Rebecca would have no one to leave all that wealth.

Ariel would have been a better choice anyway because she had already made plans for all that money. Still, to succeed, the young woman had taken love out of the equation.

Max attracted her like no other man before. Nevertheless, Ariel liked the idea of getting the trust fund more. The money wouldn't have lied to her and wouldn't have cheated on her. She could control it and make it do what she wanted, not the other way around.

"Earth to Ariel," Max said, waving his fingers in front of her eyes.

Ariel looked up at him, a little lost in her thoughts. She needed a few seconds to realize that she had forgotten about his presence and started dreaming.

"Wine would be good," the woman said quickly to deflect any questions the man would have thought to ask. "If you have some red wine, it would be great," she smiled at him thinly.

Max searched her face carefully for a few moments. The woman had seemed so deep in her thoughts that he could have sworn that Ariel had forgotten about him.

The man didn't care for her smile either, but then he shrugged and said in a light tone of voice, "Your word is my order, milady."

He left with supple steps, and Ariel stuck her tongue out behind him. That man had a real talent to say things that should have sounded complimentary, but his tone made them sound like pure mockery. She didn't care for that talent at all.

After a couple of seconds, the man's voice came from outside the kitchen.

"Aren't you coming too, Ariel? I think we'd be more comfortable in the living room."

'*Ugh,*' the woman groaned, realizing that she had also forgotten about his proposition to continue their discussion in the other room.

Ariel clenched her fists and stomped toward the kitchen door, furious that she was behaving like an idiot.

CHAPTER NINE

Ariel took a seat on the sofa and smoothed her skirt over her thighs. She needed to busy her hands with something, feeling somewhat under a microscope. Max watched her with hawk eyes, and the woman couldn't stop thinking that he was looking for any faux pas she might make.

A grin tucked at the corner of his mouth, Max came to Ariel, bringing her a glass of red wine and a paper napkin.

The man didn't see the need for that. However, he had good eyes and had noticed that a napkin always accompanied a glass of wine in the high-end lounges or cocktail bars. Max didn't doubt that Ariel would patronize such an establishment.

The woman took the glass and napkin from his hand, sketching a thin smile, and nodded. Max tried to assess the green light in her eyes, but he didn't reach any conclusion. The woman kept her secrets under lock and key and remained as elusive as ever.

"I meant to tell you," the man said, lounging in an armchair. "You look fantastic with short hair. You look good before that too," he waved his hand in a circle. "But right now, you look really sexy. The bangs emphasize your green eyes and the lines of their face," he pointed out.

"Thank you," Ariel replied from the tips of her lips with annoyance. The woman couldn't be sure that the man didn't mock her.

Even Ariel didn't know what to believe about her new image. She still needed to get accustomed to her short hair and the lack of weight over her neck.

Besides that, the man's words made her feel uncomfortable. After all, Ariel had spent a lot of time trying to get rid of Max in that past. It seemed awkward to accept any compliments coming from him.

To pass over that moment, the woman lowered her gaze to the glass she was holding and sipped some of the tarty liquid. "This is good," she appreciated the taste with a nod.

"I thought you would like it," Max agreed quietly and took a mouthful from his glass, as well. "So, are you going to tell me what I should expect to happen from now on?" the man attacked the subject he wanted to discuss after a couple of seconds.

Ariel, who was just drinking some more of the cool wine, practically choked. She spluttered for a few moments and then asked in a squeaky voice, "What do you mean?"

Max bit his lower lip, not to burst into laughter. He immediately realized what the woman thought. The man needed a few more seconds to answer without revealing his mirth.

"You called me to come and get you from work because you had car problems. You made a few comments about alarms and how someone could disable one. I can guess that you are concerned because of something. I am sure that there is more to this story than a faulty car," Max explained matter-of-factly so that the woman could get a clearer picture of his intentions for the moment.

"Oh, that," Ariel sighed with relief. "I understand now," she laughed, and Max read embarrassment on her face.

"Yes, that," Max pointed out with amusement. "What did you think I was talking about?" he asked, tilting his head to the right. The man considered that he had gained the right to make a bit fun of Ariel after all the time she had treated him like he was a low-life thug.

Ariel fluttered her hand at a loss of words. The woman didn't intend to flatter him by revealing what she had thought when Max asked what he could expect from her. The man didn't need to know anything about her feelings or her idiotic attraction to him. He wouldn't have let her live it down.

"Nothing," Ariel managed to say. "I didn't think of anything," the woman clarified, and then she brought her glass to her mouth to gain a few more seconds.

"Well, then," Max shrugged. "Tell me about the car and everything else when you are ready. It's not like we have anywhere else to be tonight," he pointed out in a mean tone of voice.

"It isn't necessary to get snarky now," Ariel retorted, brushing her bangs to the side. "I have got enough on my plate without your nastiness," she explained.

Max curved his left brow and watched her from under his lashes. The woman couldn't stop herself noticing the thickness and length of those lashes.

Catching herself in the act of admiring the man once more, Ariel cleared her voice and continued, "Well, you might think that I am reading too much in what happened. I understand if you are reluctant to continue helping me after I tell you everything."

"Maybe, you should tell me what happened first, and then I will tell you what I think," Max replied, waving his hand in a sign of invitation to begin her story.

Ariel fidgeted a little, trying to find a more comfortable position on the sofa. Then she leaned forward and left the glass on the table. The woman clenched her hands together and wetted her lips, and then she started talking, her eyes fixed on her laced fingers.

"A few months ago, I started finding flowers on my front steps," Ariel said with a brief hesitation in her voice. "I used to love red and white roses, you know," her eyes darted to Max for a few moments and then returned to her hands. "I can't stand them now," she shook her head in dismay. "Of course, I would always find a note with the flowers. Brief and printed on a piece of paper, it read, '*From your secret admirer,*' the woman explained, and her fingers shook.

Max sensed the need to sit next to her and take her in his arms but resisted. He didn't think that the woman would welcome such comforting gestures from him, so he drank some more wine instead.

"Go on," the man invited her in a quiet tone of voice when Ariel didn't continue.

The woman looked up at him for a second and then turned her eyes to her lap again. With a nod, she continued, "At the beginning, it seemed amusing. You know, getting flowers like that. I didn't think much of it," she shrugged. "Then, I started finding messages on my answering machine at home, and I began freaking out."

"What did the messages say?" Max inquired, his eyes zeroed in on the top of her head. The woman looked down, and he couldn't see the expression on her face or her eyes.

Ariel darted her eyes at him briefly and then clenched her hands harder. She knew that the problems would start now. That was where the police had stepped back, insinuating that she made a mountain out of ant-hill.

"They remarked on my looks in the beginning," she shrugged. "Then, there were brief observations of my comings and goings..."

"And...?" Max waved his hand encouragingly.

"Well, it might not seem much at first sight... Still, I felt that the person leaving those messages was following me around. He was stalking me... you know," she explained in a defensive tone of voice, expecting that Max would laugh at her for her silliness.

"It might not seem much, but it is clear that the person stalked you if they knew where you were going and when you returned home," Max said matter-of-factly, and the woman snapped her head to attention.

Ariel hadn't expected that the man would believe her. There had never been too much lost love between them. Max had all reasons to take advantage of the situation and laugh her out of his house.

Max pretended not to notice her reaction and continued, "Are we talking about a man or a woman?"

"I suppose it is a man," Ariel replied with some hesitation. "I mean, it sounds like a tin voice, but I have the feeling that it is a man."

"All right, then. Have you called the police?" Max inquired.

"I did call the police," Ariel nodded. "I told them about the flowers and the messages."

"That means that they are investigating," Max concluded.

"Not really," the woman shook her head, and her bangs bounced, attracting the man's eyes for a moment.

"What do you mean?" he asked then, a frown between his brows.

"They said that I exaggerated, and there was no reason to investigate. The messages didn't seem threatening, and after all, anybody can leave flowers on people's stairs," she shrugged.

"Are you kidding me?" the man exploded. "Do you mean to tell me that they didn't even bother to investigate?"

"Yes, indeed," Ariel nodded, watching the man with curiosity.

His outburst told her a lot. She had always sensed passion in Max, although the man had never acted on that passion. He preferred calm and rational approaches, and his present behavior seemed out of the ordinary.

"Even when I pointed out that the messages had become too... knowledgeable, you know, they still didn't think that there was a need to do some investigations. They said that until the man had done something, they couldn't look into that," Ariel waved her hand and shook her head. "I mean, you know, it's stupid to wait that something happens. At least, that's what I think. I wouldn't find any comfort in the thought that they investigated after something happened to me," the young woman pointed out, putting her hand on her chest.

"Of course, you wouldn't," Max agreed with her. "That's beyond stupidity," the man shook his head with astonishment. "I would have expected something more from our police," he noted out. "Couldn't you get another police officer to look into this story?"

"Not really," Ariel shook her head. "When something happens, you have to go to the police station in your neighborhood. It is not like they have a lot of officers to deal with these matters," she shrugged, opening her arms and putting her hands up.

"Yes, I can understand that," Max nodded with disappointment. "I think I'd like something else to drink," he said, looking at his glass of wine. "I feel like something with more punch to it," the man pointed out. "What about you?"

"I am all right with this," Ariel took her glass off the coffee table and wetted her lips.

"Good then," Max slapped his hands over his thighs and then rose to get a glass of whiskey.

The woman watched his supple gait with a sigh. That was why she always tried to avoid being in his vicinity. There was something in that man that put her system in override. She didn't know if his built or his way of moving was the culprit, but she could hardly keep her hands off him.

Max returned and sat in the same armchair. He took a good mouthful of his drink and then groaned.

"This stuff is good but very strong," the man explained to Ariel. "Anyway, let's go on. You said that the messages showed that the guy knew too much. What do you mean?" he asked.

"He started mentioning the people I met during the day and what I wore. He knew a lot of things about how I spent my days. For instance, he knew about the wedding yesterday. You know, Lily and Mark," she mentioned, although she wasn't very sure that he knew about the marriage. She hadn't seen him at the wedding the day before.

"I see," Max frowned.

"After a couple of disturbing messages yesterday and this morning, I decided to cancel the contract for my landline," Ariel explained. "He would always leave his messages there."

"Good thinking," Max approved.

"Not really," Ariel sighed.

"What do you mean?" the man watched her with puzzlement.

"Well, I did cancel the landline. The very next moment, the guy started calling my mobile phone," Ariel threw her hands in the air with exasperation. "I didn't even know that he had my mobile phone number," she shouted in frustration.

"That's a problem, yes," Max agreed, concerned about the substrate of that discovery. "So he called you on the cell phone today?"

"Yes, twice. Once to rant about my office outfit," Ariel said with a flutter of her hand.

"Your outfit?" Max looked at her in befuddlement.

"Yes," Ariel confirmed. "Apparently, I am dressed like a prostitute. He said that I shouldn't show the goods to anyone but him," she grimaced, but Max could see the fear in her eyes.

The man didn't doubt that Ariel had reasons to be fearful. Her stalker didn't seem to mince words and showed signs that he was escalating.

"I see," Max said. "I can understand why such a thing would distress you. It's beyond creepy, to be honest. And the second time?"

"Well, he called, but I didn't answer. I refused to check my voicemails," the woman confessed. "Then, I found that note under the windshield wiper, and that scared me witless," the woman admitted with a grimace.

"Have you kept the note?" Max rose from his armchair swiftly and leaned over her.

Instinctively, Ariel drew back a little, and the man raised his left brow.

"Don't tell me that you're afraid of me," he tilted his head inquiringly.

The woman shook her head with vehemence. "No, of course, I'm not. Your move just surprised me," she explained her reaction.

"I see," the man said. "Well, do you still have that note?"

"Yes, it's in my purse," Ariel frowned. "I thought I'd better keep it for the police if they want to look at it," she added with bitterness in her voice. "I doubt that they would, but…"

"I can see why," Max patted her shoulder. "So, where's the note?" he asked.

"It's in my purse, which I left in the kitchen," she replied and tried to stand up.

"Don't bother," the man stopped her. "I'll bring the purse to you," he turned and headed to the kitchen.

Ariel widened her eyes and watched him leave. The man hadn't seemed so assertive before, and suddenly, she saw him in a different light.

"I think you might have gotten a new voicemail," Max mentioned when he got back. "Your phone was ringing when I got to the kitchen but stopped now. I didn't think you'd like it if I answered your phone," he handed the bag to Ariel.

"Thank you," Ariel nodded. "That's considerate of you," she noted.

"Aren't we both extremely polite this evening?" Max observed with mockery in his voice.

Ariel slashed him with a withering glance but didn't reply. She took the phone out of her purse and checked the missed calls, frowning.

"Yes, he has already called twice," she informed Max. "He left a voicemail every time," the woman sighed deeply.

"I'm sorry, baby," the man rubbed her shoulder. "You'd better put the voicemails on speaker. I'd like to hear what he said."

"But I wouldn't. I mean, I don't want to hear what the man said," Ariel retorted with petulance.

Max grinned and shook his head. "I can understand that. However, we need to know what's going through his mind. If you want, I can listen for myself," he stretched his hand toward her, asking for the phone.

"If you insist," she grimaced and handed him the phone.

Max accessed the voicemail. "I need your pin," he looked up at her.

"Oh, yes, I forgot about it," Ariel shrugged and gave it to him.

Max listened to the voicemails, and his face darkened. His dark coffee eyes turned to slits, and the metallic light in his pupils stole the woman's breath away.

"Is it bad?" she asked in a small voice.

"It is not good," the man shook his head. "Anyway, don't worry. I won't let him get to you. We'll devise something to keep him away from you for good," he promised in a grim tone of voice.

"How?" Ariel inquired, and her tone betrayed her lack of confidence.

The police hadn't helped her at all, after all. She didn't expect that Max would be able to do more than they had done.

"Don't worry, everything is under control," Max patted her shoulder again. "Where's the note you found under the windshield?" he asked her.

Ariel rummaged through her bag and took out the crumpled note. Max read it and didn't like it at all.

"All right, I will be honest with you so that you know what to expect," Max looked straight into her eyes.

Ariel nodded, even though her heart sank into her boots. She didn't expect that the man would give her good news.

"I set the alarms everywhere," Max said, waving his hand to encompass all doors and windows. "I also set up a backup one. Now, I understand that the guy knows his way around the alarms, and I expect he would be capable of disarming the first alarm. If he does, he should set off the second one. However, if the man is good and knows his business, he might be able to disarm my backup as well," Max explained. Then he noticed that all color drained from the woman's face.

"Do you mean to tell me that he might get inside?" Ariel asked in a high-pitched tone, and her hand flew at her chest.

"Yes, he might," Max replied somberly. "You need to be ready for that, so I can't lie to you only to keep you calm. Do you understand that?" the man insisted, looking intently into her eyes.

Ariel swallowed hard and nodded.

"Good, then," Max approved. "We will need not to give him any clues about where you are going to sleep. From what he said in the voicemails, I gather that the stalker had already surveyed the house. The guy knows that we spent some time in the kitchen. He also mentioned that he saw us moving into the living room."

Ariel looked around the room with scared eyes and started to rub her hands with apprehension.

"Ariel, look at me," Max ordered forcefully, and the woman's eyes snapped back at him.

"Yes, your stalker surveyed the house. Now, he knows in what rooms we've been so far. That doesn't mean that we can't do something to deter him. We can stop him. First, I'm going to draw the curtains here," Max strode to the wide French doors and pulled the dark red curtains closed. "When we go upstairs, I will go through all the rooms and pull the curtains everywhere. Thus, he won't know in what room you will sleep," he explained and then searched her face attentively. "I hope you understand that you have to sleep here tonight, Ariel. I have a chance to protect you here, but if you want to go home alone, I can't offer too much help," Max pointed out.

"I know that," the woman admitted grudgingly. She didn't like the idea of staying with him over the night, but she didn't have any other solution.

"All right then," Max nodded. "You'll sleep alone in a room, but we will take a few precautionary measures before that," he reassured her.

CHAPTER TEN

Ariel couldn't fall asleep. She lay in bed and listened to the noises of the night. The young woman had always found it difficult to sleep in a new hotel room or when she went to visit friends for the first time. Now, besides that, the fear kept her tensed, as well.

The young woman didn't know what to do. She believed that Max would try to keep her safe. The man seemed determined about that. Still, that took care only of that night. Ariel couldn't move in with him, and once alone at her place, she didn't know what she could do to protect herself.

Her brother didn't seem to care about what happened to her, which was somewhat expected. They might not share the same looks, but they shared the same outlook on life and the people around them. Ariel could hardly find guilt with him.

The other men she could trust to help her were away and didn't come back for several days. Still, Ariel knew that she couldn't afford to stay with Max until then.

Determined to make her great-grandma happy, Ariel couldn't get involved with Max. Misleading the man might have been a solution. However, the young woman didn't think that she could do it without guilt. Ariel had been at the other end of the stick in the past. She knew that it felt awful. The woman couldn't do it to another human being without remorse.

Besides, Ariel liked Max in her way. She experienced a strong attraction to the man. The woman had little doubt that she would have succumbed to that chemistry if she had lived with Max, even if for a few days.

Ariel hadn't been in a relationship for a couple of years. She had tried a few times after breaking up with Eric, but every relationship ended in disappointment. Now, the young woman craved attention and human touch, and she was afraid that Max would prove too difficult to shake if she got involved with him.

Furious with herself and the circumstances, the young woman groaned and punched her pillow with exasperation. Then, she buried her face in it, and the fresh smell of the pillowcase tickled her nose.

She felt good in the bed Max had provided. The room didn't smell stale, and Ariel wondered if Max had the habit of ventilating all the rooms every day. He couldn't have used all of them all the time.

The size of the place had astonished the young woman. Max didn't seem the kind to have a four-bedroom house. Ariel would have pictured him in a loft somewhere or maybe in a mobile home, always ready to move on.

His dark looks reminded her of a nomad gypsy, but seeing him in that habitat ruined some of her misconceptions. Ariel liked to be right all the time, or at least, most of the time. It seemed that she had lucked out with Max. None of her early impressions turned out to be true.

The young woman shook her head, exhausted. The last few days had been a rollercoaster of emotions for her with Lily's wedding and her stalker's messages. That evening spent with Max had also taken a toll on her.

Ariel hugged the pillow in her arms. The woman burrowed even more under the comforter despite the warmth in the room.

Max had given her one of the bedrooms at the back of the house. The noises of the street rarely insinuated into that room. They seem to come from afar and didn't bother Ariel at all.

The comfort surrounding her put a smile on her lips. The idea that she was indeed protected was the last conscious thought the woman had before surrendering to slumber. Exhausted, Ariel slid into sleep with a light sigh.

No light penetrated the heavy curtains covering the windows. In the distance, a raccoon turned a garbage bin upside down. However, only a vague echo of the racket reached the woman's ears. Ariel turned on the other side with a light sigh and curled under the duvet.

The young woman dreamed of white trails in a park and curious squirrels perched on leafless branches. A strong arm supported her, and when she looked up, her gaze burrowed into the darkness of Max's eyes.

A loud crash in the hall, followed by a shout of pain, prompted Ariel to wake up with a startle. She sat up in bed, shaken to the core. The woman pressed her hand over the mouth to muffle any sound that might have escaped off her lips.

Max had advised Ariel to hide in the walk-in closet if anything happened. However, the woman forgot everything about it and stayed still, frozen in the middle of the bed.

CHAPTER ELEVEN

Taut like a bow, Ariel clenched her fists over her mouth. A few seconds later, the sounds of a scuffle from outside her door pumped adrenaline into her veins. Her heart pounded in her chest at every groan that bounced from the corridor walls.

Tears burned in her eyes, but Ariel knew that she couldn't let them fall. The woman was afraid that she would start sobbing uncontrollably, and the people in the hall would hear her.

Suddenly a body hit the wall near her bedroom door, and a cry flew off her lips. Ariel bit her lower lip to stop herself. An inhuman shout preceded another thump, and the woman imagined that someone fell to the floor. She waited for something more to follow, but silence stretched.

Ariel panicked, not knowing what she should do. She didn't know if Max was the one on the floor, and she doubted that she would be safe in the walk-in closet if the other guy would start looking for her.

The woman shook but decided to bite the bullet and got off the bed. She started to the door but quickly remembered the lamp on the nightstand. Ariel unplugged it quietly and wrapped the cord around her hand.

On tiptoe, she headed to the door again. There, she leaned forward and listened. A heavy breath came from the hallway, and the woman chewed her lips, unsure of what she should do.

She pondered on the situation for a few seconds and concluded that she was screwed anyway. At least, being the first to attack would help her gain a few seconds.

Ariel opened the door with a sudden move and launched herself out into the corridor. With a warrior shout on her lips, she raised the lamp to crash it in the head of the attacker. A strong arm blocked her motion.

"Are you trying to bash my brains in?" Max asked in a morose tone of voice. "That guy has already done a good job," he informed her. "You don't have to pile on that."

"Oh, my God, you're all right," Ariel exclaimed, and then she let her tears fall, happy that Max couldn't see them because of the darkness of the corridor.

"More or less," Max mumbled and then moved away from her, thinking to get to the switch and lighten the hallway. "I thought that I had told you to hide into the walk-in closet," the man observed, turning on the light.

"Yes, you had," Ariel replied with a small voice. "But I didn't know who won the fight out here, so I preferred to see and try to protect myself, depending on the situation," she continued with a shrug.

"So much for your confidence in me," Max noted with sarcasm, turning toward her. "Yes, it's true. I might not have been the one standing in the end, but at least, I tried," he waved his right hand.

Then, Ariel noticed the stiffness of the man's left arm and the trail of blood on his chest and the floorboards.

"Oh, my God, you are hurt," she shouted from the top of her lungs.

With a grimace, Max covered his right ear with his palm and closed his eyes tight. "Well, good, you want to finish the guy's job," he observed dryly.

"What the heck are you talking about?" Ariel asked, heading with quick steps toward him. "You're badly hurt, you idiot."

"I could live without the insults, though," Max retorted. "I will be fine," he waved his healthy hand and then went to lean over the man on the floor. "I think we should call the police. This guy might come to his senses soon, and I don't feel like starting to fight again," the man said, glancing at Ariel.

"I'll go and take my phone to call," the woman nodded and hurried toward the bedroom. "You keep an eye on him," she threw over the shoulder.

"Duh," Max mumbled. "As if I hadn't known that I should be doing that," he pursed his lips.

Ariel returned with the phone in hand after a few seconds.

"Have you already called?" Max raised his eyes to her.

"No," she replied. "I don't know the address."

"Ah, that's true," Max nodded. "Call in, and I'll give you the address when they ask for it," he advised her, turning his eyes back to the boy at his feet.

Ariel made the call and then slid down along the wall. Her legs didn't support her anymore. "It's been a long, crazy day," she murmured.

"I agree," Max replied, watching her from the corner of his eye. "But at least you have got rid of your stalker," he pointed to the man who started stirring.

Max punched the man in the temple with a casual move, betraying no rush, and the man groaned briefly and stopped fidgeting.

Ariel bit her lower lip and then asked, "Was it necessary?"

"I think so," Max raised a shoulder. "I don't have too much fight left in me," the man admitted. "I don't know if I can hold him back if he came to."

Ariel nodded after a brief hesitation. His words made sense in a way. Anyway, the woman didn't want to face the attacker all by herself. If Max was out of the fight, she wouldn't have anyone to help her.

CHAPTER TWELVE

The police came in less than five minutes, and they brought an ambulance with them. Ariel had told them about the fight between the two men when she called. She had also mentioned that there were some casualties.

"So, with all those alarms you set up, the man still got inside," one of the officers observed, while two others handcuffed the intruder and took him out to the police car.

The paramedics had already checked the attacker and declared him fit to be taken to the police station. Besides a few severe bruises, a swollen eye, and a cracked lip, the guy wasn't seriously hurt.

Now one of them cleaned a deep cut along Max's arm. The man had already refused to be taken to the hospital. He didn't consider that it was paramount to have the wound treated right then.

"Yes, he did," Max nodded. "And he does know his job," he observed. "But for the addition of the laser security system, which is operated separately from the other two, the man would have probably succeeded in what he wanted to do."

"Is the laser system silent?" the officer inquired.

"Yes, it is," Max replied. "The alarm is quiet and sounds directly into a device on my nightstand," he explained.

"Why so many alarms?" asked another officer.

Max shrugged and said, "It is my specialty."

"Interesting," the first officer noticed. "What do you do for a living?"

"Ah, I'm not talking about what I am doing now," Max waved his right hand, stealing a look at the paramedic who was studying the cut on his left arm. "Is anything wrong?" he asked the EMT expert.

"You need sutures, sir," the man replied. "It's too deep, in my opinion."

"Just put some bandage over it," Max said. "Stitches are not necessary," he expressed his opinion.

"But sir…"

"I can't go to the hospital now," Max interrupted him in a harsh tone of voice. "I need to stay here," he added, and his eyes darted toward Ariel.

The woman clenched her hands, trying to keep her agitation under control. The green of her eyes lit the paleness of her face, and Ariel chewed her lips absent-mindedly. She seemed tense and overwhelmed because of everything that had happened that evening.

Hearing the man's words, the young woman glanced at him. Now, she noticed that the EMT was fighting with Max over his wound and understood that she needed to intervene.

"I will go with you," Ariel chimed in, and Max looked at her with curiosity. "You need to have stitches," she said in a stronger voice. "You seem reluctant to leave me here alone, so I will go with you," the woman reiterated, even though the thought of stepping into a hospital gave her chills. She always avoided visiting anyone in there.

However, she owed the man for having protected her that night. If she had been in her house alone, only God knew what might have happened.

"I will survive without going to the hospital, Ariel," Max replied dryly.

The man had already noticed that the idea of going to the hospital nauseated the woman. He knew that sometimes it was difficult to get over some phobias, regardless of how stupid they seemed.

"But now you don't need only to survive," the woman retorted in a mean voice. "I said I would go with you, and I will," she threw him a shriveling glance.

The man shrugged and nodded. "So, we're going go to the hospital," Max said to the paramedic. "Once I've finished with the police here," he pointed to the officers who patiently waited for him to make a decision.

"We'll finish immediately," one of the officers assured him. "Do you know the intruder?" he asked.

"No, I haven't seen him in my life," Max shook his head. "Anyway, he wasn't here because of me," he explained.

"But why then?" the officer asked, looking at him with puzzlement.

"It seems that my friend, Ariel, has been stalked for a while," Max said, waving his hand toward the young woman.

"Have you spoken to the police about this stalker?" the second police officer inquired, turning to the woman.

"I tried to," she replied in a haughty tone of voice.

"Tried to?" the other officer raised his brows.

"Yes, I tried to," Ariel repeated, stressing every word. "They told me that I was exaggerating, and they couldn't do anything for me."

"And I'd like to know how the police could tell something like that to a young woman. So, she comes to you complaining that she has a stalker. She shows you the proof, and you just brush her away," Max tilted his head, watching the police officers through narrowed eyes.

At that moment, Ariel likened him to a pirate. His dark looks and incandescent dark eyes brought pain to her chest. Max looked too good to be true.

"I apologize, miss," a red-faced officer hurried to say. "I apologize on behalf of my colleagues, and we will look into that. Could you give me the details of what you told them, please? I need to put them in my report, and we need them when we process the man we arrested."

Ariel nodded and quickly gave them all the details she remembered. The young woman handed them the note she had found under the windscreen wiper earlier. She also offered them the use of her answering machine to listen to some of the intruder's last messages.

"Have we finished here?" Ariel asked afterward. "We need to go to the hospital," she pointed out, glancing at Max.

"Yes, we have," the officer nodded and shoved his notebook and pen into a pocket. "We'll keep in touch. However, you shouldn't worry anymore, miss. That man won't get near you again," he reassured Ariel.

Although she knew that Max was responsible for her being safe again, the young woman thanked the police officer in a hurry, and she turned to Max afterward.

"Do you want to go by ambulance, or do you want me to drive your car?" Ariel asked.

Max looked at Ariel and then glanced at the paramedics, asking for their opinion.

One of the medical experts intervened. "You'd better go to the hospital by ambulance, and the doctor will see you at once. You won't have to go through extensive triage because we have already done all that here. Your friend can follow by car. She can meet you there," the paramedic advised.

Max wanted to refuse, but Ariel put her hand on his arm.

"Go with them, Max. I'll come after you in your car. Just let me know where the car keys are," she asked him.

The man sighed deeply and then accepted. He led everyone downstairs, where he dug his car keys out of a bowl and handed them to Ariel.

"See you at the hospital," she said, and impulsively, she leaned toward him and kissed his cheek.

The man's left brow hiked up his forehead, and his eyes zeroed in on her face. A rosy powder spread over the woman's face and neck, and the man's lips twitched.

Max liked how Ariel looked at that moment, slightly embarrassed and disheveled. He had never seen her like that. Usually, the woman seemed cold and untouchable. Her hair looked groomed to perfection, and she never appeared ruffled.

Seeing her blushing was reassuring. It showed that the woman had feelings. He could work with that.

CHAPTER THIRTEEN

Max also hated hospitals and doctors. He had had his share of medical care during his crazy years when he used to defy the odds and threw himself in daredevil adventures. Consequently, he didn't like it when he lost control over his body, and a doctor would tell him what must be done.

The man didn't mind seeing blood on someone else. He did hate the sight of blood when the blood belonged to him. He also wasn't too keen about having his skin prodded and poked.

Impatient, Max waited for the doctor to arrive and paced the small space. Ariel had followed him in the treatment room and watched him moving to and fro.

"Does it hurt?" the woman asked him, noticing his nervous steps.

Max turned to her with an unreadable light in his eyes. He brushed his fingers through his hair and shook his head.

"What kind of question is that?" the man asked her. "I wouldn't be here if it didn't hurt, would I now?" the man retorted in a harsh tone of voice.

"I am sorry," the woman turned her eyes to the floor.

"Why would you be sorry?" Max frowned. "You didn't hurt me," he pointed out, upset that the woman believed that she was at fault.

"But if it hadn't for me, you wouldn't have been hurt tonight," Ariel replied in a small voice.

"Don't be stupid," he ordered harshly. "As if having you hurt would have been better," Max said in a grim tone of voice.

Ariel wanted to say something more, but the doctor entered the room and looked at the two young people with puzzled eyes. The man felt the charge in the atmosphere and wondered if he shouldn't have come earlier.

"Is everything fine here?" the doctor inquired, waving his hand to Max and inviting him to take a seat on the edge of the hospital bed.

"Yes, everything is fine," Max replied in a tone that didn't broach more probing and then sat on the bed.

"Let me see your arm," the doctor asked, deciding to forget about what he had felt when he entered the treatment room. The doctor didn't like the brief answer of his patient either but decided to let it slide.

As Max feared, the man poked and prodded, making him grit his teeth.

"We'll clean it, and then I'll stitch it in no time," the doctor promised, feeling the tension in the man's body.

"All right then," Max replied through his clenched teeth. "The faster, the better," he added, hoping to leave the hospital soon.

"I'll be fast about it," the doctor said, and then he went out of the room to bring a nurse with the supplies he needed.

Max shook his head, seeing that the man was leaving. "Why didn't he come with everything he needed from the beginning?" he wondered, standing up and starting pacing once more.

"Maybe he didn't know what he needed," Ariel commented.

"The paramedics told the triage nurse what was what. That nurse also saw my arm," Max contradicted Ariel. "He should have known what to expect and not waste time with unnecessary exams," he concluded.

"He will be back soon," Ariel replied to him in a soothing voice. The man sounded irritated, and she didn't want to aggravate him even more.

"You are afraid to poke the bear, Ariel, aren't you?" Max noticed with amusement in his voice. "Don't worry, I won't bite you, even if you contradict me," he patted her shoulder.

The woman narrowed her eyes to slits but bit back the words that popped onto her tongue. She was aware that Max was the only thing that had stood between her and her stalker that night. The least she could do was to humor the man for a while.

Max watched her with curiosity and shook his head. "I always knew that you are something else. You are not a simple woman. I might not like everything I see in you, but one thing is damn sure, girl. You are far from boring," he said with a shake of his head.

"Are you trying to annoy me?" Ariel asked him in a clipped tone of voice.

"Not really," Max replied. "I am just honest about what I think. Would you prefer that I lied to you?" he tilted his head, gazing at her inquiringly.

"Of course not," Ariel hurried to say. "I always prefer to know the truth. Anyway, it doesn't really matter," she waved her fingers.

"Why?" Max curved his left brow. "Because I am not important enough?" he guessed.

"I have never said that," she retorted heatedly. "I am just saying that this night will pass. We won't see too much of each other afterward."

"And why not?" Max asked, sitting on the edge of the bed.

He blamed his sudden weakness on the blood loss, but he knew that the shock of hearing Ariel denying him any future contact was the reason he felt so shaky.

"Because it is not wise," Ariel said, turning her back to him. The woman looked out of the tiny window even though she couldn't see anything but a gray wall.

"Who says it is not wise?" Max insisted. The man didn't like to be told what to do, and besides, he had never learned to let things go.

"I say it is not wise," Ariel turned back to him, and the green in her eyes burnt holes in the man's face. "We are different. We come from different backgrounds. There's no future for people like us," she explained with agitated gestures.

"We are different," Max agreed with her assessment. "And we come from different backgrounds for sure. I can't deny that. But that doesn't mean that there is no future for people like us. Look at Becka and Bryan," he pointed out.

"They might be an exception to the rule," the woman didn't give up. "I, for one, don't believe that they will last."

"You might not like me," Max said quietly. "It's your right. But you lie to yourself if you believe that Becka and Bryan won't last. They make one of the most solid couples I have ever seen, Ariel. I know you don't like Bryan. I don't know why, but that doesn't make their marriage less solid only because that's what you hope," he continued in a harsh tone of voice.

Ariel wanted to reply, but she stopped when the door to the treatment room opened. The nurse came in, pushing a cart, and the doctor followed her.

The following twenty minutes passed with difficulty. Ariel couldn't take her eyes from the doctor's movements even though she felt her dinner in her throat. Once again that evening, all color disappeared from her face, and even her lips looked a pale pink.

Max tried not to look at what the doctor was doing and focused on the posters on the walls. The man had already learned every word on those posters by heart when the doctor finished stitching his arm.

"You will need to keep this arm dry for about five days," the doctor advised Max. "You can shower if you cover it with a plastic bag or something. I will give you a prescription for antibiotics," he added and started filling in a page on a prescription pad. "I will prescribe some pain killers, as well. It will hurt some," the doctor shrugged.

"You don't need to prescribe painkillers," Max waved his fingers. "I have good tolerance to pain, and I never take anything stronger than ibuprofen. I hope it is not a problem if I start the antibiotics tomorrow. I'm thinking of having some whiskey tonight. That would help with the pain as well," the man winked at the doctor.

The nurse shook her head, but the doctor laughed.

"Yes, you can wait for the antibiotics until tomorrow," the man nodded. "But don't drink too much. You lost enough blood to make that combination unsafe."

"Nah, don't worry. One glass, or two, the most," Max reassured him. "So can I leave now?" he inquired.

"Yes, you can. You should go to your family doctor after seven days to have your arm checked. If you feel any discomfort or see red and inflamed streaks, come back to the ER," the doctor advised him in a grave tone of voice.

"I understand," Max nodded and then picked up his jacket to get dressed.

The nurse and the doctor left the room, and Ariel closed the door behind them after saying thank you. When she turned back to Max, she noticed that the man was trying to put on his jacket, but his arm didn't help him too much.

"Let me help you," Ariel strode to him with hurried steps.

"It isn't necessary," Max stopped her, putting up his hand. "I won't die until I get home if I don't wear the jacket. It is warm in the car," he said and started to the door.

"But it's cold outside, and you'll freeze until you get to the car," Ariel rushed after him.

Max waved his hand in the air and continued along the hall toward the exit with wide steps.

"You don't even know where I parked the car," Ariel said from behind him, and the man stopped.

"All right," Max agreed. "You show the way," he invited her.

CHAPTER FOURTEEN

Ariel drove back home, but only after they shared a heated discussion in the parking lot. Max didn't want to allow her to handle his car, and the woman didn't even think to put her life in his hands when he had only one that he could use without restrictions.

"I know you're upset with me right now, Max," Ariel said apologetically. "If you want, once we get back to your house, I can call a cab and go home," the woman shrugged, thinking that the man had tried her patience enough that night. She could do with some respite for the moment.

The man snorted but didn't dignify her words with a reply. Ariel gritted her teeth in frustration, throwing Max a scathing glance. She would have liked to pay him back in kind.

The woman even thought to punish him by casting one of the spells she should have had in her arsenal on him. However, Ariel was afraid that her inability to control her witchcraft, combined with her fury, might lead to disaster.

119

Ariel wanted only to make Max pay a little, not to turn him into a grub. The woman sighed. She couldn't use her powers, knowing that she might get things wrong. Still, she needed to do something if she wanted to keep her sanity.

The young woman wasn't a very patient person in her good days anyway. However, right then, at the end of that nightmarish day, she was already at the end of her rope.

She had tried to stay calm, keeping in mind that Max had put his life on the line for her. Nonetheless, Max made it more and more difficult for her to be grateful to him. Ariel had to bite her tongue a few times not to yell at him.

"What does that mean?" the young woman asked in a grim tone of voice, looking fugitively at him sideways.

"Just that I think that you've lost your mind," Max replied matter-of-factly, waving his fingers dismissively.

Ariel sighed deeply to control her temper and shook her head. The man was getting on her nerves, and the impulse to pay him back became powerful.

The woman thought of her sister. If Becka had been in her place, Max would have already blown away by a terrible storm. The man was lucky that Ariel hadn't inherited those talents.

"Look, Max. We don't seem to get along too well tonight," the woman observed primly. "Maybe it would be better if we weren't stuck together in the confinement of a house."

'Or I might turn into a lunatic and throttle the life out of you,' Ariel continued in her mind with ferocity.

The young woman felt she was upset enough to overcome Max, even though the man towered over her and weighed at least fifty pounds more. At that moment, her fury gave her the power she needed.

Ariel pulled air deep into her lungs, and then, she tried to explain patiently to Max, "There is no danger out there for me now. I do appreciate everything you've done for me tonight…"

"This is bullshit, and you know it," Max retorted angrily, leveling his harsh gaze on the woman's face. "What you mean is that you don't need me anymore. Feeling safer, you want to go back home so that you don't have to lay your eyes on me any longer."

"You are right about one thing," Ariel replied heatedly. "I don't want to lay my eyes on you right now because I feel like throwing something at your hard head," she shouted, glancing at him furiously. "I've already told you that I'm grateful for everything you did for me. I tried to help you in the hospital, Max, and you threw a tantrum in front of the doctor like a toddler…"

"A toddler?" Max spluttered, and the thunder in his eyes ignited.

The man couldn't believe his ears. No one had ever accused him of behaving like a snotty child.

"Yes, a toddler," Ariel didn't back down. She even thumped her hand on the steering wheel to drive her point home. "You are an adult. You should behave like one. I understand you're hurt, but that doesn't mean…"

"It's not about me being hurt," Max retorted heatedly. "It's about you thinking that you can write me off when you don't need me anymore."

The man sensed that he wasn't entirely fair. That discussion had only started because he didn't like the thought that his arm stopped him from driving. Afterward, Max tainted that annoyance with the idea that Ariel didn't think much of him and couldn't wait to get rid of his presence.

The man knew that he was right at some level. Despite that, he was also aware that he had extrapolated everything, making things worse. Still, he didn't feel like apologizing for his words and poor attitude.

"Look here, champ," Ariel burst out in an angry tone of voice, losing the last drop of patience. "I'm no Florence Nightingale. That's true. But I still wanted to help you through the night and be there for you because you helped me. If you can't get that through your thick skull, then the problem is yours, not mine. I don't want to spend the rest of the night sparring with you," she warned him.

"You don't want to spend the rest of the night with me, period," Max noted. "Don't you think that I know what your opinion of me is? You made it quite clear every time we met," he turned to her to drill his point home.

"That's got nothing to do with what's going on here," Ariel retorted, keeping her eyes on the road with stubbornness.

"Oh, but I think it does," Max said in a quiet tone this time. "All right, I might have behaved a little out of character tonight, but you did behave precisely the way you did every time we were thrown together."

Ariel shook her head and fought not to let her tears fall. She had wanted to do something nice for him, and Max had managed to turn everything around and make her look selfish.

"All right," she said in a controlled tone of voice. "I'll stay at your place tonight, but tomorrow morning, I'm gone," her palm slashed the air between them.

The woman couldn't leave him alone after the man got slashed because of her. Ariel wouldn't have forgiven herself for such selfishness ever.

"Suit yourself, princess," Max replied in an indifferent tone of voice and took his gaze off her.

The man turned his eyes toward the window to show Ariel that he didn't care. However, his mind got busy. The man started looking for ways to make the woman remain with him even when the morning came. It was his only chance to make her see him the way he was, and Max had stupidly almost blown that chance off.

"I usually do," the woman didn't miss her chance to have the last word.

They spent the rest of the trip in silence. Ariel hoped that the night would pass soon enough so that she could get rid of Max for good. The last few hours had exhausted her.

No matter how good-looking the man was, he didn't worth the trouble. His stubbornness would have made her run away even if her grandma had liked him. Ariel preferred men that were more amiable and catered to her whims. Max didn't fall in any of the two categories.

Max also had to contend with his black thoughts. The man felt used and discarded.

He hadn't helped her so that Ariel could show her gratitude to him. He would have done the same for any other woman.

However, he had hoped that the woman might warm up a bit toward him. The man had tried his best to charm Ariel during the last year and a half. Still, he didn't get too far with her.

When they arrived at his place, Max went directly to the bar concealed in a niche in the living room and poured a glass of whiskey. "Do you want some?" he turned toward Ariel, but the woman shook her head.

"I've had enough excitement tonight, thank you," Ariel spat her words. "I expect that I will sleep like a log. I don't need any help for that," she tilted her head toward the glass in the man's hand.

"Suit yourself," Max shrugged. "I think it is good medicine, taken in small doses," he explained.

The man sipped from his glass and hissed through his teeth. A well-aimed fist had cracked his lips, and the burn of the alcohol took his breath away.

"Look," he gazed straight into her eyes afterward. "I know that our conversation got derailed tonight. It might have been because of built-up frustration, or maybe because of the aftermath of an adrenaline infusion," the man shrugged. "I didn't mean to offend you, and I don't want that you go to bed angry with me."

Ariel considered Max carefully and realized that the man apologized to her in his own way. That didn't make everything right, but she was willing to get back to the status quo and forget about their dispute. After all, the woman had promised herself to do her best not to be in the same room with him too soon. She could survive for one night.

"Don't worry," Ariel waved her hand with nonchalance. "I have already forgotten," she smiled thinly at Max, barely curving her lips.

'*Yeah, I bet you have,*' the man thought bitterly. Max hadn't missed the lack of smile in the woman's eyes.

Now, the man scolded himself quietly, knowing that he had had his chance with Ariel, and he had blown it.

"Do you need help to take out your t-shirt?" Ariel asked Max to put an end to any other possible discussion.

The man looked at her and grinned. Ariel grimaced, realizing what kind of thoughts crossed his mind.

"I like your offer, baby, but I think I will sleep in it tonight. I don't feel like going through the motions to take it off," Max explained to her, waving the hand with the glass. "However, I will take your offer in the morning if it still stands," he winked at her.

"The offer to help you take your t-shirt off will still stand. Don't confuse that with something else, though," Ariel warned him sternly, determined to settle things once and for all.

"How could I?" Max replied with bitterness. "You've made it very clear that you don't want to have anything to do with me, haven't you?"

"Here we go again," Ariel rolled her eyes, sick of rehashing the same things all over again. "You know what? I'm going to bed," the woman announced Max in a matter-of-fact tone of voice. "I'm exhausted, and I can't go through this once more," she added and headed toward the door.

"Yeah, I got that," Max mumbled behind her, but his words reached Ariel, and the woman gritted her teeth in frustration.

No matter what she did, she would always find herself on the wrong side with that man.

With a grim look on his face, Max watched Ariel leave the room. Then, he drained the content of his glass in one go. That very moment, the man hated himself.

'You're stupid, man. You could have gone about it differently. Who knows, you might have made the woman warm towards you,' Max shook his head in dismay.

The man glanced at the bottle of whiskey and thought of pouring another glass.

'This is not the answer,' he decided after a few seconds and put his empty glass on the coffee table.

A few moments later, Max went upstairs to try and sleep for a while. He doubted that he could, though. The pain combined with his restless thoughts seemed to be the perfect cocktail to keep him awake that night.

CHAPTER FIFTEEN

When she went downstairs early the following morning, Ariel found Max in the kitchen. She stopped for a moment, unsure of what she should do next.

The man glanced briefly at the young woman. The shadows under his eyes told Ariel that Max hadn't slept too much that night. Her heart cringed at that thought, but the woman tried not to show any compassion, afraid that she would start the conversation from the night before. She didn't feel like going through that again.

"Morning," Max greeted her in a morose tone of voice, and although he cracked a smile, Ariel noticed that his eyes remained somber.

"Good morning, Max," Ariel replied quietly. "You didn't sleep too much, did you?" she inquired, feeling bad for him.

The man shrugged. "I have time to sleep later today. I've already called and announced that I wouldn't be going to the dojo for the day. Would you like some coffee?" Max turned his back to her and started making the coffee.

Ariel hesitated for a moment. She wasn't very sure that she wanted to spend too much time in his company that morning. The previous night had already exhausted her.

"Have you decided already?" Max asked the woman, without turning back to her. "I can assure you that I won't bite even if I didn't sleep too much last night."

The young woman grimaced but then shrugged. "Yes, why not?" she replied, thinking that she did need a cup of coffee after sleeping so little. Ariel hoped that the potent fuel would help her to kick off her day.

"Then take a seat at the table," Max invited her, tilting his head in the direction of the corner kitchen table. "The coffee will be ready soon, and I have already put some croissants in the oven," he informed Ariel.

"Do you also bake, like Bryan?" the woman asked him in a puzzled tone of voice, and her brows hiked high on her forehead. The coincidence would have proved too much for her.

Max burst into laughter and shook his head. "Sorry to disappoint, sweetheart," he managed to say through guffaws of laughter. "Bryan is one of a kind. I'm afraid you lucked out," he turned toward the woman, a grin on his lips. "I don't cook or bake, and I have no intention to learn in this lifetime. I can live with eating out or buying take-out just fine."

"But you have just said…" Ariel started to say, but Max interrupted her with a wave of his fingers.

"I know what I said, but that doesn't mean that I am the one who baked the croissants. I just bought some pre-packaged pastry, ready for baking. That's all," the man explained, raising a shoulder. "I can read the instructions on the package and turn on the oven. I don't need to do more than that."

"Oh, I see," Ariel nodded. "Well, I understand that they are good, as well," she said with studied indifference. The woman didn't want to let him know that she was an avid buyer of such pre-packaged food.

"That they are," Max agreed with her assessment. "Maybe, they're not as good as Bryan's, but good enough," he shrugged once more.

Considering that they had milked that subject dry, Ariel headed to the kitchen table and took a seat on the bench. She sighed deeply and leaned back to let her tension seep away. At the same time, her curious eyes watched Max take two mugs out of the cupboard.

Do you take sugar in your coffee?" the man asked without turning his head toward her. However, he felt her steady gaze on his back between his shoulder blades.

Max barely managed to control himself and not to fidget. The man didn't want to let Ariel understand that she could unnerve him. He was already at a disadvantage in front of the woman because of his feelings for her.

"Yes, I do," Ariel replied in a quiet tone of voice.

Subdued, the woman folded her hands in front of her on the top of the table. The man's constant presence in her life during the last sixteen hours had played havoc on her system.

"Milk?" Max continued the interrogation.

"Yes, if you have some," Ariel nodded, although she knew that the man couldn't see her motion.

A few moments later, Max came to the table with a mug for her. "I'll bring the sugar and milk at once," he informed Ariel and turned to make good on his word.

"I can help, you know," she stood, ready to go and bring the other things to the table.

"It's not necessary. I manage," Max waved her to sit back on the bench.

Ariel pursed her lips but then grabbed his right hand swiftly. "Max, don't be absurd. I can't sit here, waiting for you to bring everything to the table. I can use both my hands, and I won't die if I put everything on a tray to carry it here. I know that you think I am self-conceited, but I can assure you that I have done this before," she said in a rush, and the green light in her eyes glinted.

Ariel wasn't the type of woman to fool herself. She had noted the man's attraction to her, but she had also noticed that he kept his eyes open and didn't gloss over her so-called flaws. That she didn't consider them failings was another matter altogether.

Max measured her determination for a few seconds and then nodded. He didn't wish a repeat of the last night's fiasco. The man wanted to make some progress with the woman, not to alienate her for good.

"All right, then. Knock yourself out," Max invited her, showing to the kitchen counter where he had already gathered what they needed for their breakfast.

Ariel shook her head and hurried to put everything on a tray and bring it to the table in one go. She set everything on the table and then turned to see what Max was doing.

He had already taken the croissants out of the oven and tried to transfer them on a plate now. However, with only one functional arm, the man didn't have too much success in his endeavor.

Ariel noticed his frustration, and with another shake of her head, she headed toward him immediately.

"I think you should take the coffee to the table. I will put the croissants on the plate," Ariel offered in a soothing tone of voice.

Max glanced at the woman and pursed his lips. "It seems that I can't do too much with this stupid arm," he spat the words out of his mouth.

"I know it looks like that now, but it will pass," Ariel reassured him, patting his right hand. "And soon, Max, don't worry."

133

The woman was afraid that Max would call her out for all those platitudes, but the man contented himself to offer her a tight grin. Then, he snatched the carafe filled with coffee and headed back to the table. However, every step the man took proved his irritation and frustration with the present situation.

Ariel felt sorry for Max. The woman didn't want to take a closer look at her feelings toward him. However, she did care for the man in her way. Besides, Max wouldn't have been in that situation if he hadn't tried to protect her.

Guilt gnawed at the woman, who knew that she should offer to help him for a day or two. Max couldn't use his left arm without pain, and his motion range was limited.

Still, regardless of her guilty feelings, Ariel knew that she couldn't do it. Spending too much time in closer proximity to Max spelled danger. She had already wasted too much time thinking of him after every one of their encounters in the past.

That very moment, Ariel felt the man's dark eyes on her, and her body temperature had already taken a hike. She couldn't risk remaining there with him.

The young woman returned to the table with the croissants piled up on a plate. She put them next to the coffee pot and said in a light tone of voice, "They do smell good, Max. I love having coffee and croissant in the morning," Ariel added, taking a seat opposite to Max.

Then, she poured coffee in one of the mugs and doctored the hot liquid with sugar and milk under Max's curious eyes.

"I wouldn't have penned you for a woman that loves so much sugar," the man observed.

Ariel shrugged and said, "I like sugar and sugary things as much as the next person."

"I can see that," Max pointed his chin toward the woman's mug. "I don't," he explained. "Not very healthy, you know."

"It might not be," Ariel said in a negligent tone of voice. "But it works for me," she ended the discussion, biting into a croissant. A moment later, she covered her mouth and started puffing.

"What the heck, Ariel?" Max frowned, jumping off the bench, ready to snatch her.

The woman put up her hand to stop him. After a couple of seconds more, she swallowed and then said, "Sorry, I was just stupid. I didn't realize that it was too hot," Ariel said in a remorseful tone of voice.

Max shook his head. "I thought you were choking. My first thought was that I might not have enough strength in my left arm to perform the Heimlich on you," the man explained angrily, and his eyes smoldered with fury and resentment.

"I am sorry," Ariel repeated contritely. She trained her big green eyes, framed by thick lashes, on the man's eyes to charm and disarm him. His behavior tickled her, but she didn't want it to go further than that.

135

"No big deal," Max mumbled and sat back on his spot. "Don't do it again," he ordered in a grim tone of voice to save face.

The man was not stupid and knew when he was played. However, he decided to give her the points for the moment.

"I won't, boss," Ariel replied, lowering her glance to the tablecloth, and her voice reflected the smile curving her lips. She knew that she had won that round.

They continued to drink their coffee in silence, munching on the croissants and stealing furtive glances one to the other.

"I am curious about a thing," Max said suddenly, and the woman's head snapped to attention.

"What's that?" Ariel inquired, looking at him with puzzlement in her eyes.

"What don't you like about me?" the man burst out.

Max had thought to ease into that subject, but at the last moment, he forgot everything about it. It was a sore subject for him, and he wanted to clear the waters. After all, he needed to know whether he should hope for things to change or not.

Ariel opened her mouth to answer, but no sound flew off her lips. She cleared her voice to gain some time and then said, "I have never said that I don't like you."

"Not in so many words," the man mumbled his agreement with her statement. "But you show it all the time. It's like you can't stand to have me around at times," he added, and his words sounded like an accusation.

"I'm afraid that you misunderstood," Ariel chose her words carefully, trying to reason with him. "It's not that I don't like you, or I can't stand being around you."

"Then what?" Max insisted, determined not to let her hide behind words.

Her eyes cast downward, Ariel brushed a finger on the rim of her mug, thinking how to explain everything.

"I like you just fine, Max," she said. "That's not the issue here," the woman pointed out, glancing at him.

"Then what?" the man repeated his previous question, staring at her with hard eyes.

"We're not good one for another," the woman shrugged.

"How have you figured out that?" Max asked sarcastically. "It's not like you have gone out of your way to spend any time with me," the man pointed out. "An emergency had to occur for you to look at me otherwise than with annoyance."

"Look, Max," Ariel replied. "First of all, let me repeat what I told you last night. We come from different backgrounds, and I mean very different backgrounds," the woman emphasized her words.

"That we do," Max agreed with her with a nod. "That doesn't mean that things wouldn't work between the two of us," he leaned forward to give more weight to his words, gazing straight into the woman's eyes.

Ariel stared at him for a few moments and then shook her head. "No, they wouldn't," she contradicted him. "Max, you don't have a clear idea about how different we are. You know practically nothing about my family and me, so you can't have an accurate idea," she pointed out.

"I know enough," Max waved his hand, discounting her assessment. "I'm good friends with Matt and Jay, after all. Bryan is my friend and partner," he mentioned, proving his point.

"And that's all you know," Ariel raised a shoulder disparagingly. "Things are a bit more complex than that, though."

Max tried to contradict her, but the woman raised her hand. "Look, Max, believe me, I am in the right here. I don't really know what you expect from a relationship between the two of us, but I can tell you right now that you would be disappointed. I stopped believing in love and being in love some time ago. That's for teenagers, who haven't tasted life yet. I know better than that," the woman explained in earnest.

Max stared at her without blinking. He couldn't believe her words. "Do you mean to say that you don't believe that two people can get together and love each other?" the man raised his brows high.

"That's what I'm saying," Ariel nodded. "I thought I was in love once, but now I know better. Still, I was disappointed when I understood that I also didn't represent anything else but the means to an end for my so-called lover," she explained with bitterness.

"How do you know you weren't in love?" Max wondered. "People often convince themselves of the opposite if that helps them to cross a difficult period," he explained. "Still, you can't accurately say that you weren't in love," he shook his head.

"Believe me, Max. I know for a fact that I wasn't in love. And after that failed relationship, I decided never to get involved with someone else pretending that such feelings exist," the woman reiterated her position.

"No, no, no," Max stopped her, and exasperation penetrated his tone of voice. "I need to know what proof you have to make you think that it wasn't love what you felt. How can you be so sure? Usually, people have a lot of doubt over that."

"Well," Ariel started to say in a hesitant voice. "There are things you don't know, as I've already told you."

"Then help me to know those things," Max insisted.

"Sorry, Max," Ariel shook her head, but her voice didn't betray any contrition. "I can't tell you anything. It's a family secret that it's revealed only in certain circumstances, and that's not the case here. Anyway, the result of such confessions would probably be that you would invite me to promptly leave the house. So, I think that it's better if you don't know," the young woman shrugged. "And I know what I'm talking about," she pointed out so that the man wouldn't contradict her. It has happened to me before," she confessed. "With that guy, I told you about."

"Now, you really need to tell me everything," Max insisted, his curiosity reaching new levels.

"No, I don't have to tell you anything," she replied in a petulant tone of voice and frowned.

"Because you think that I would react like that douchebag?" Max inquired, leaning toward her.

"Partly, maybe," Ariel admitted hesitantly, and insecurity slid in her voice. "However, there are rules, and I don't like to break the rules. Besides, we will never get to the point where I need to confess anything to you, so we'll better drop the subject."

"You'll tell me," Max stated with confidence. "I will wear you out."

"Not if I am not here for you to do it," Ariel contradicted him.

"Do you want to bet?" Max grinned at her.

"Max, believe me, it's not worth it," Ariel put her hands up. "I like you. It would be difficult not to like you, of course. You're a very handsome guy, and you know it. You have these dark looks and a mysterious aura. I am sure that almost all women you meet fall for you. However, I can't offer you anything more than a brief physical relationship. Nothing more," she pointed out, and the man's brows curved up his forehead in puzzlement.

"That's... bold," Max noted, not sure that he had chosen the right word to express his opinion.

"That's honest," the woman retorted, correcting his assumption.

"So, you'd be comfortable to have a physical relationship with me," the man summed her words, and a smile perched on his lips. He liked that new development in their conversation.

"A brief one, yes," Ariel nodded. "But because my grandma doesn't like you and doesn't want me to get involved with you, I won't have one," the woman explained matter-of-factly.

"How old are you? You're thirty, thirty-two?" Max asked in an incredulous voice, frowning slightly.

"You're close," Ariel replied haughtily. The woman never liked talking about her age, which was a sore subject for her.

"So, does your grandma still choose your playmates at this age?" Max inquired with sarcasm.

Embarrassed and miffed, Ariel blushed, and her fingers shook with repressed anger.

"As I mentioned earlier, things are more complex than that, Max. I told you that you don't have the entire picture. Anyway, what's important for you to know is that I've already lost too much. I don't afford to lose anything more," she tapped with the tip of her index finger onto the top of the table to drive her point home.

"Like what?" Max curved his brows once more.

"Like money," the woman admitted but blushed violently.

She sensed that her words might not sound quite right. People always disliked the ones who chased wealth at the exclusion of anything else.

Max shook his head with disappointment. He had expected anything else but that.

"Even you seem to know that it doesn't sound quite right," he observed with bitterness. "Anyway, if money is what you love most in this world, you are free to chase your money," the man stood and took his mug to the sink. "I'm not going to stop you. I don't think that anyone could stop you. After all, everyone has the right to achieve their dreams," the man continued in a flat tone of voice.

Max didn't seem to care about it anymore. He headed to the door, avoiding looking at Ariel.

"I'm going back to my room now. You can call a cab and go home, Ariel. The door will lock automatically behind you," he informed the woman.

Ariel regretted that she had caused so much pain. The man tried to hide it under the indifference he displayed, but the woman didn't buy it.

"Max...," she tried to say something, but the man shook his head to stop her words and passed by her without a single glance.

"Have fun with your life, Ariel. You'll need it," he said quietly on his way to the stairs.

'Money rarely keeps you warm when you need it,' Max mumbled for himself.

"You will need my help to take your shirt off," Ariel hurried after him. "I am here to help you. You must know how grateful I am to you for everything you've done for me," Ariel implored him.

Max turned around, and his hard eyes zeroed in on her face. "I don't need your gratitude. It's the last thing I would ask from you," he said in crisp words.

The man took two steps toward the door, but then he turned his eyes back to her. "I don't need your help for anything," Max declared without emotion. "I'll just tear the shirt off. Go home, Ariel. It's no use to waste your time with the likes of me," he dismissed her.

"I never said...," Ariel tried to explain.

"And I won't give you a chance to say it," the man replied in a harsh tone of voice. "I've got my pride. I'm done running circles around you. Find another idiot," Max advised her. "Now get out of here," the man shouted at her.

143

Then, Max turned his back to her, went toward the staircase, and started up the stairs.

Frozen to her bones, Ariel watched him climb the stairs. When the man reached the landing, unshed tears burned the woman's eyes.

CHAPTER SIXTEEN

In the days following her abrupt leaving from Max's place, Ariel was torn between sudden thoughts of him and moments of frustration and anger. The man knew how to raise her hackles.

If she felt anything for Max, the young woman stubbornly denied her attraction to him. She glossed over it by concluding that she was only grateful for what the man had done for her.

Most of the time, Ariel kept busy so that she wouldn't think of the man and what had happened between the two of them. She didn't have to try too hard.

The police visited her at home a couple of times. The first to come were the officers who answered her call when she started receiving the messages from her stalker. They came to apologize and ask for more details to build a case against the man.

Ariel couldn't refrain from pointing out that their previous assessment of the situation had proved wrong. The officers might not have liked it but tried to show contrition for their haste in dismissing her fears.

When the police visited her the third time, the police officers also informed Ariel that the man had been charged with home invasion. They also explained that his case was in the prosecutor's hands right then. They explained how the trial worked without getting into details too much. However, Ariel did have a high intelligence quotient and could read between the lines.

Ariel saw red before her eyes when the police divulged the fact that the stalker had got out on bail until the date of his trial. She couldn't believe her ears.

The officers assured her that the man would not inconvenience her anymore because that would not help his case. They explained to her that the surety would monitor the attacker constantly. Thus, the man wouldn't be able to do anything.

However, the young woman had a hard time believing them. She didn't need to watch action movies or read crime books to understand that, regardless of the surety, the man would be able to do whatever he wanted.

Ariel went further and checked what the punishment would be for the man's crime. Afterward, she concluded that the guy wouldn't have anything to lose if he breached his bail conditions and came after her. The punishment might be the same, even if Ariel ended up raped or dead.

The young woman was apprehensive of what the future might hold in store for her. Then, she started thinking about ways to protect herself.

During the entire day after the departure of the police officers, Ariel came up with various ideas. However, she discounted them one after another. Fortunately, she had the time to do it.

That morning, the woman had felt under the weather. When she looked out of the window while drinking her coffee, the grey of the sky had depressed her, so she called in sick.

Ariel hadn't believed that she could go through with her work that day. Her job annoyed her more and more, and the young woman had thought of changing jobs more than once.

Fortunately, because she had stayed at home, Ariel had the time to ponder on possible ways of action while cleaning the house. That she didn't have any success in finding a valid one was another matter.

Ariel remembered that she had installed an alarm system a few years back, but she was a practical woman. She knew that that didn't mean that she was out of harm's way.

The woman's run-of-the-mill system wouldn't have been too much of a challenge for someone who knew what to do. Her stalker had shown that he had good skills when it came to disarming such devices, and hers wouldn't even turn out to be a challenge for him.

Then Ariel thought of leaving Toronto for a while. Still, she didn't know where to go and how to go about that. The young woman liked to organize her life almost to the second, so she found it difficult to leave somewhere at short notice.

Vacations for her meant plans made months in advance. The woman organized every outing during those vacations beforehand, and that took hours of preparation.

She couldn't just buy a ticket somewhere without having anything planned in detail. Ariel couldn't even bear the thought that she should give up proven good habits, only because a maniac wouldn't forget about her.

Ariel didn't want to ask for help from Max again. Not only was the woman peeved because the man had asked her to get out of his house, but she didn't feel that she had the right to ask anything from him.

After all, she had told him that she didn't see any possible future for them together. Her honesty came back to bite her now, and the woman scrunched her nose at that thought. Maybe it would have been better if she kept her mouth shut for a while, even though that meant to deceive the man.

The thought of approaching her brother, Alex, also crossed her mind. Still, the young woman didn't believe that she could withstand another crass rejection from his part, so she put that idea aside. To keep her sanity intact, Ariel decided to go there only if she couldn't find any other way out.

The woman finished cleaning the en-suite bathroom in the master bedroom. Then she started on a thorough cleaning of the second bathroom on the first floor. All the while, she kept coming up with various ideas and rejecting them.

Discussing matters with her father or uncles didn't even make the list of possibilities. Ariel saw them as old people, although she admitted that the men didn't look too bad for their age. Still, the woman didn't think that the men would be able to fight an aggressive attacker. She had never seen them fighting, and in most circumstances, they kept their cool and tact.

Ariel thought of Matt and Jay, but she knew that her cousins wouldn't be back until the following week. Feeling dejected, she dared thinking of Bryan, who, usually, would have been the first on her list. The man had the necessary skills to confront an attacker. Bryan was also her sister's husband, so he might have been felt obliged to assist Ariel.

In the beginning, the young woman hadn't wanted to approach Bryan because of his relationship with Max. However, the man was the best second option if Ariel couldn't count on Max, and she couldn't.

Ariel had just finished with the kitchen when she realized that Becka and Bryan must have already returned from their vacation. The woman ran to get her mobile phone off the coffee table and call them. She thought that it wasn't too late, and she could go to visit them that evening.

She picked up the phone and noticed the blinking light on the screen. Her eyes widened with horror when Ariel realized that she had just got another voicemail, always from an unknown number.

'*Not again, damn it! Not again,*' she mumbled, and fear overwhelmed her.

The woman started shaking, and the phone fell off her shaky fingers. With dismay, Ariel tried to catch it but missed. On the way down, the cell phone bumped into the corner of the coffee table. Then, it changed direction and hit the leg of the armchair next to the sofa.

The young woman flinched when an ominous bang accompanied the last leg of the phone's trip. Ready to scream because of her frustration, Ariel leaned over the table to get the phone. Then she noticed the crack on the screen, and a furious shout emerged from her mouth.

"This is not possible," the woman started crying afterward.

At first sight, the phone seemed to have turned off, and she tried to turn it on. It didn't work. Ariel shook her head, unnerved. She couldn't believe that she was so unlucky.

For a few moments, the woman couldn't gather her thoughts and decide what to do. She merely looked at the broken mobile. A feeling of doom overwhelmed her, and her brain refused to function.

Suddenly, Ariel glanced at the French doors of the living room. The man could be out of those doors, ready to come and get her. She needed to do something and soon.

Ariel jumped to her feet when she realized that she was a sitting duck for the stalker if she remained there, prone in that state. The woman ran out of the living room and up the stairs.

The fear gave her a new purpose, and she swiftly changed in a pair of jeans that had seen better days. The woman wore those pants only to garden, but she didn't even think of that. For the first time in many years, Ariel didn't care how she got dressed. She pulled an old pullover over her head and took the first pair of boots her eyes laid on. She didn't even notice that the ankle boots didn't match her pullover.

She ran downstairs, snatched her bag and car keys from the small table in the entry hall, and continued running to get to the door that opened to the garage. There, Ariel stopped. She didn't know what she could find on the other side of the door.

Chewing her lower lip, Ariel turned various scenarios in her head. The stalker might have waited for her in the garage, and in that situation, she would be in severe trouble. On the other hand, the man might not have managed to get rid of the person monitoring him yet. In that case, Ariel had a fighting chance to get out of there.

'Anyway, I have to go out,' Ariel concluded. She couldn't remain in the house alone. *'I need something to protect myself,'* she mused.

The woman thought of the knives in the kitchen, but she discarded that idea at once. Ariel didn't believe that she would have the courage to stab a man.

'But I'm pretty sure that I could bludgeon him… Maybe not to death, but hard enough so that he wouldn't budge afterward,' she concluded.

Now only if she could find something that would serve that purpose… Ariel bit her nails, making a list in her head with the objects that seemed suitable to that purpose.

Going through what she had in the kitchen, she remembered that her aunt Marjorie had given her a rolling pin when Ariel moved into the house. Marjorie had hoped to teach Ariel to cook, but the young woman turned out to be very recalcitrant to that endeavor.

Ariel decided that the rolling pin was a perfect choice. *'I can have a good grip, and it is easy to handle,'* she thought on her way to the kitchen. *'If only I could remember where I put it,"* the young woman scrunched her nose, looking around.

She excluded the suspended cupboards from her search. There she kept her dishes, some cereal boxes, and other things that she used almost daily. Her gaze fell on one of the cupboards farther from the stove and kitchen counter.

'It must be there,' she nodded. *'I don't remember to have ever opened that cabinet,'* Ariel murmured while rushing to see if the rolling pin was in there.

The woman sighed with relief when she found it among some pans and pots. She picked it up and tried to feel its weight in her hand.

'Yep, good weight center,' she concluded. *'It will work if I need to hit something or someone with it,'* the woman grimaced, not very keen to try that theory. Her stomach got upset when she saw the guts of a fish. To crack a man's skull open wasn't on her wish list.

Then, Ariel ran out of the kitchen and back to the garage door. She put her ear to the door and held her breath, listening carefully. She didn't hear anything. Contented, the woman opened the door slowly. She leaned forward to verify the interior of the garage without getting inside.

Nothing seemed out of the ordinary, and Ariel pushed the door completely open. Her eyes swept the entire area for a few moments, and then the woman ran to her car.

Luckily, the mechanic had had what he needed to fix it at the car service, and he had returned it to her a few days ago.

Ariel wasn't a religious person, although most of her family was. Still, she said a brief but sincere prayer when she turned the key in the ignition. The woman feared that the stalker had already got to her car. Then, she would be stuck there without any means of communication.

However, the engine purred, and Ariel released the air she involuntary held in her lungs with a loud whoosh. The woman opened the garage door, using her remote, and then she drove out. The urgency to see Bryan had become more immediate. The man had to help her. If necessary, Ariel would remind him that she was his wife's sister, and he wouldn't have a choice.

CHAPTER SEVENTEEN

Ariel drove at the higher speed limit all the way to her sister's house. She threw fearful glances in her rearview mirror all the time. At every traffic light, her eyes swept over the people in the cars stopped in her proximity. The woman also looked at the people walking on the pavement. She wanted to make sure that no one was surveying her.

The traffic was pretty light for a Friday evening, but Ariel had the feeling that she didn't move fast enough. Driven by sheer fear, the woman didn't think she would arrive at her destination in one piece.

'Pull yourself together, Ariel,' she grumbled after she had avoided an accident in the nick of time. *'The idea is to get there, not to land into the hospital or into the morgue,'* the woman encouraged herself.

The trip to her sister didn't take more than fifteen minutes, but Ariel was a total wreck when she arrived there. Usually, she would glance into the rearview mirror to check her make-up and hair, but this time, she checked if anyone was following her.

Ariel stopped the car right in the driveway, even though she could find an available parking space in the street. However, she didn't want to have to walk a too long distance to the door. Before getting out of the car, she picked the rolling pin first and then her handbag.

'Priorities change,' the woman noticed with a shrug. *'And people say that I'm not adaptable enough,'* she snorted.

Although only five meters separated her from the flight of stairs to Becka's door, the woman didn't take any chances but ran there faster than ever before.

Ariel stopped on top of the stairs to catch her breath for a couple of seconds. She pressed her left hand on her midriff, trying to regulate her breathing. The short running distance hadn't stolen her breath, but the fear pulsating in her chest had exhausted her.

The door opened suddenly in front of her, exactly when the woman decided to ring the bell. With a distressed cry, Ariel raised the rolling pin over her head to defend herself. At the same time, she closed her eyes. A powerful arm intercepted the improvised weapon.

"I knew you disliked me, but I've never thought you'd try to bash my brains in," a deep, amused masculine voice reached Ariel's ears.

Startled, the woman sighed and opened her eyes. She knew that voice well and would have recognized it in any circumstance. After all, she had heard many times in her restless dreams for the last sixteen months.

Ariel was right. Max stood there, in front of her, his gaze searching her face. In less than a second, the humor disappeared from the man's eyes. The nude distress signs on the woman's features didn't leave room for interpretation , and he knew that something had happened to her.

Gently, Max took the rolling pin from her hand and gently pulled her toward him. "What's wrong, Ariel?"

Without thinking, the woman threw herself at the man's chest and burst into sobs. Max grimaced when her sudden motion jarred his arm, but then he handed the rolling pin to Bryan, who had stopped behind him, and slid his right arm around the woman's back.

"What the heck is going on here?" Bryan asked Max, and his voice sounded very angry.

The man had known Ariel for some time now, and he had never seen the woman lose control or shed a tear. His sister-in-law was tough as nails and would usually show the weakness and compassion of a hyena. Bryan had never thought that Ariel would be capable of strong emotions, or that she could express them by shedding any tears.

Bryan had come to blows with Ariel several times in the past. The woman loathed his marriage to her sister and had never made a secret of that. She considered that man belonged to a much lower social class. The young woman had stated more than once that Bryan could hardly be seen as anything else but a thug.

Indeed, Ariel and Bryan had had their disagreements. Still, that didn't mean that the man didn't feel a sort of responsibility toward her. The woman was his wife's sister, and Bryan had adopted that family as his the moment he pledged his heart to Becka.

Ariel burrowed more into Max's chest, and this one shook his head to Bryan, mutely asking him to stop his questions for the moment.

"Let's go inside," Max proposed, and with a nod, Bryan drew back to let them pass by him.

The man waited for Max to bring the woman inside and then closed the door behind them. He waved his hand toward the kitchen, and Max led Ariel in there.

Becka came out of her office, curious to see what the commotion was about. Her sister's sobs had made her forget about organizing the materials she prepared for her new semester at the university.

"What happened?" Becka asked with astonishment in her voice. The woman hadn't ever seen Ariel cry like that. Not even when Eric turned out to be a lousy toad, her sister didn't carry on that way.

"Let's talk in the kitchen," Bryan proposed and took his wife's hand in his, pulling her after him.

When the couple entered the kitchen, they noticed that Max had already helped Ariel to sit down. The man was now brushing her bangs away from her wet face, whispering soothing things in her ear.

Bryan pushed Becka in front of him, inviting her to sit down. The woman sat in a chair on the opposite side of her sister. Then, the man laid the rolling pin on the table and stared at it with astonishment.

"A rolling pin, Ariel?" he asked, and the disbelief in his tone of voice was unmistakable. "Seriously?" the man exclaimed.

By now, Ariel had calmed down a little. She shrugged and wiped her face with the back of her hands.

"That's the only thing I could think of," she confessed. "I had a choice of knives, but I knew that I wouldn't be able to use them," the woman answered to him.

Bryan shook his head, not sure that he had understood her words correctly.

"All right, let's try with another question," the man sighed. "Why do you need a rolling pin? I don't believe that you wanted to hit Max over the head because you couldn't have known he was here," Bryan pointed out.

"Of course, I didn't want to harm Max," Ariel shouted, outraged. "Why would I hurt him? Just because he can be a jerk when he wants?" her voice raised a couple of octaves, and immediately, the woman cringed, realizing she had turned into a shrew.

The expressions on the other people's faces strengthened that impression.

"How come I am a jerk?" Max intervened, upset to hear her words.

"You threw me out of your house," Ariel shouted, pointing her finger to him accusingly, and Becka's brows hiked high on her forehead.

Ariel was fast in her anger, but she would usually keep a glacial demeanor. She wouldn't shriek like a *commoner*, as she would have labeled that behavior.

"That's a story I need to hear," Becka murmured to Bryan. Max didn't seem the kind of man who would throw a woman out of the door.

Her husband squeezed her hand and nodded. "I do too," he whispered back to his wife. "But let's be patient for a moment," he urged Becka.

Then he turned his gaze toward Max, who stared Ariel down with a frown.

"Do you have anything to tell me, Max?" Bryan asked his friend and partner quietly.

"Possibly," the man raised a shoulder without taking his eyes from Ariel.

"Why just *possibly?*" Bryan stressed the word in a harsh tone of voice, staring Max down at his turn.

"It depends on Ariel," the man explained, pointing his chin to the young woman. "She decides what I may tell you," he continued, staring at Ariel to see what she wanted him to do.

Ariel stared back at him for a few seconds and then nodded. "I think you'd better tell him what happened. Then I'll add the rest," she said in a resigned tone of voice.

"The rest?" Max shouted angrily, looming over her. "What else happened?" he wanted to know. "Tell me!"

Ariel sighed and shook her head. "Let's take it chronologically," she asked him. "You tell Bryan about what happened before, and then I'll tell you about today," the woman proposed a compromise.

The man's lips became a thin line, and he braced his fists on his hips. He assessed the woman's features for a few moments and then turned to Bryan.

Max told Becka and Bryan everything that happened after he had answered Ariel's call. He gave them all the sordid details, inclusively the final quarrel he had with Ariel.

Becka and Bryan listened quietly, although their reactions to the man's story were very different. The woman's eyes widened, and her lips parted because of the shock. Bryan controlled himself better, but the rigid line of his shoulders betrayed his fury.

When Max got to the reason for the spat he had had with Ariel, Becka shook her head in disbelief.

"Oh, God, Ariel! You don't think that grandma will just hand you her money," the woman exclaimed. She didn't know what to believe about her sister's claim that only the love for money counted.

"She might," Ariel replied with fire in her eyes. "You refused it, as well as Matt. Rebecca won't offer anything to Jay and Lily, so it stands to reason that she might choose someone who respects her wishes," the woman explained. "Like me!" she concluded, pointing her thumb to her chest.

"Let's not talk about this aspect anymore," Bryan touched his wife's hand to stop her from continuing that discussion. Becka looked incensed enough to rip a new hide to her sister. "Ariel is entitled to her own opinions," the man nodded to the young woman. "What we believe about them doesn't matter."

"That's right," Ariel approved his words. "It's my life and my choices," she pointed out, tapping her index finger on the tabletop.

"All right then," Bryan tried to calm her. "Let's talk about this stalker of yours," he proposed, fixing Ariel with his grave gaze. "He was arrested, I understand."

"Yes, that night," Max answered, squeezing Ariel's hand. "The police took care of him."

"Not really," Ariel intervened, tossing her head.

"What do you mean?" Max turned his eyes to her. "He was arrested. I was there. I saw it," the man insisted, waving his right hand in large circles to give more credibility to his words.

"Yes, he was arrested then," Ariel nodded. "However, he made bail. The police informed me of that today," she told him.

"How the heck could he make bail after committing such a crime?" Max jumped off his seat.

The man couldn't believe that the stalker was free to move around and do whatever he wanted.

Ariel shrugged. "I don't know how, but I know he did. This afternoon, I got another voicemail," she said in a small voice.

Max gritted his teeth, and a deep frown appeared between his brows. He reached out and grabbed Ariel's slender hand, squeezing it forcefully. A yelp flew off the woman's lips, and the man apologized quietly, releasing the pressure on her fingers.

"We'd better listen to that message," Bryan chimed in.

Although he appreciated his friend's reaction, he didn't want that the man's fury escalated. He knew that Max could control his temper, but he had never witnessed what the man could do when the woman he loved was in danger. Bryan preferred not to find out just yet.

"We can't," Ariel said in a morose tone of voice.

"Why not?" Max asked snappishly, and his black gaze turned to her with reproach.

The young woman turned her eyes to the tablecloth and pulled his hand from the man's grip. Then she folded her hands in her lap, lacing her fingers.

No one said anything for almost a minute when Max, who couldn't stand the suspense anymore, touched the woman's arm.

"Ariel, what happened with the message?"

The young woman didn't answer immediately but fidgeted a few moments in her seat.

"Come on! It can't be so bad," Max snatched one of her hands from her lap to make her snap from that state.

"I got scared, all right?" she snapped at him.

"That's understandable," Bryan intervened in a soothing tone of voice. "So, what happened, Ariel?"

"The phone fell from my hand," she started crying. "It banged the corner of the coffee table and then flew into the leg of the armchair where it got smashed. I can't use it anymore," the woman said with a whimper in her voice.

"As long as you have the SIM card, we can put it in another mobile phone," Max explained to her. "So, we can listen to that voicemail," he concluded with satisfaction in his voice.

"Only if you go back to my place and pick up the pieces off the carpet," Ariel replied, raising a brow.

"We might do just that," Bryan nodded, engrossed in thought. "We'd better know what that voicemail says," he continued, glancing at Max, who approved the man's train of thought.

"And what about me?" Ariel asked, glancing from one man to the other.

"What do you mean?" Max frowned.

"Where do I fit into your plans?" she clarified.

"Of course, we'll take care of you," Max snapped. "You can't imagine that we would let you face that deranged person by yourself," he frowned at the young woman, questioning her intelligence. A smart woman would have known that they wouldn't let her fight by herself.

"I don't know what to imagine," Ariel retorted. "My brother can't be bothered with my existence. You snap at me when I refuse to have a relationship with you..." she started to summarize all her troubles when Becka stopped her.

"Alex can be a toad, Ariel. That's true. You have gone through a rough period, and it's not finished yet. But you can't put Max's anger in the same category as the others. He tried to help you, shared his hopes with you, and you just threw everything back in his face," the woman pointed out, raising her voice.

"You're my sister," Ariel glared at Becka. "You should be on my side."

"I am on your side when your side is right," Becka shook her head. "I won't take it when you behave with the same degree of empathy that Alex showed to you," she scolded Ariel, who turned red with embarrassment.

Max put his hand on the woman's shoulder and squeezed gently. "Don't worry, Ariel. It doesn't really matter what happened," he assured her. "I understand where we stand, so it's all good," the man continued.

Suddenly ashamed of her outburst, Ariel looked away. Bryan shook his head to his wife to stop any comments she might have had.

"All right," he said. "We should think of a plan, Max. If that guy is out on bail and already tried to contact Ariel, we need to find a way to protect her."

"Yes, we can't let that man get close to her," Max agreed, brushing his fingers through the woman's hair. "We'll find a way, Ariel. You needn't worry," he promised to her.

The young woman nodded but didn't raise her eyes from her hands. The man's touch felt good, and Ariel enjoyed it. She was afraid that the man could read that pleasure in her eyes, and the woman didn't want to encourage any hopes he might have had.

Ariel just couldn't give him what he wanted. She had plans and didn't want them to go to waste.

"First, we should contact the police to let them know that the guy broke the bail conditions," Bryan proposed, and Max nodded in agreement. "They will start looking for him, and we will take care of the rest."

"Let's hope that the surety has already informed them," Max intervened. "Maybe they've already begun the search. Once they apprehend him, the guy won't make bail anymore, and Ariel will be safe from him," the man noted. "At least, that's what I know," he shrugged.

"You're right," Bryan agreed with his friend. "I think we should ask your parents to keep the children for a few more days," the man turned to his wife.

Becka looked at him inquiringly, raising her brows.

"I know that we've already abused their willingness to take care of them, but it's better than having the kids here for the moment. We can't know whether the stalker has followed Ariel here or not," he explained.

Becka didn't wait for him to say anything more and pushed by him immediately to get to a phone and call her parents.

"There's no hurry, sweetheart," Bryan tried to assure her, but the woman dismissed his words with a wave of her hand and rushed out to call her mother and father.

"That's good thinking," Max agreed with Bryan. "Now, I don't know what kind of warning system you have here," the man said, looking around the kitchen as if he could have checked the system that way. "This guy knows a lot about disabling alarms," he warned Bryan. "The attacker managed to by-pass two of my alarms at home. Luckily, I also have the motion sensors, and that's how I knew that he'd broken into the house."

"I didn't pay too much attention to the alarm system here," Bryan replied in an apologetic tone of voice, looking straight at Ariel. "I didn't think it was necessary. Probably it would be better if Ariel stayed at your place for a while, and if it's not too much trouble, we could come there, too," the man asked Max. "If the stalker followed Ariel, he might try to break in here," Bryan explained. "I wouldn't want to have Becka in any danger. Besides, between you and me, we'd have more chances to subdue that guy. Let's not forget that you have only one arm available to fight," Bryan pointed out, pointing his chin to Max's left arm. The man had noticed that his friend moved it with difficulty.

"Of course, I don't mind," his friend assured both Ariel and Bryan. "I was just thinking the same thing. Ariel would be more protected in my house, even if the stalker had already learned how my warning system works. And both Becka and you are more than welcome to stay at my place," Max said, looking from Ariel to Bryan and then back.

"I hope to convince Becka to move in with her parents for a few days," Bryan said in a low tone of voice so that his wife wouldn't hear him from the other room. "I wouldn't want her in the harm's way," he explained to Ariel, who nodded that she understood.

"Good luck with that," Becka's voice came from the doorway. "If you think that I'd go and hide under my parents' bed, you're truly mistaken," the woman slashed her husband with a withering glance.

Bryan sighed deeply. His eyes darted toward his wife, and the man shook his head morosely.

"Yeah, I knew that I didn't have a prayer to convince you to stay put," he told Becka. "I am more and more convinced that you are an adrenaline junkie, pumpkin," the man added.

"Whatever," Becka shrugged. "What you need to know is that we are a team, and I won't agree with letting you risk your hide if I am not right there on your side."

"Does that mean that my hide doesn't count as long as you're not present to witness my demise?" the man commented with a thin smile on his lips.

Ariel looked curiously from her sister to her brother-in-law. She had rarely seen them getting involved in a dispute, and she didn't know what to believe.

At his turn, Max pretended to study the ceiling carefully. He didn't want to interfere between the two of them. The man believed that there were moments when he'd better keep his nose out of other people's business.

Becka slapped her husband's shoulder. "Your hide counts enough but won't worth a lot if you try to cut me out," she pointed out, and Bryan grinned.

The man liked it when the woman turned into an untamed tigress.

"Don't be snotty," the woman warned him. "We married each other for better and for worse. I'd like to keep my part in that promise," she put her nose up.

"That's... very ethical of you," Bryan said because he didn't know how to reply.

The man appreciated the woman's bluntness and faithfulness. However, Bryan would have loved Becka's attitude more if his wife had accepted to remove herself from the equation in such dire circumstances.

Becka frowned and braced her hands on her hips. She doubted that her husband's words were complimentary, and the woman seemed ready to explode.

Max considered that the time for keeping his nose out his friends' business had long passed, so he intervened in their conversation.

"Let's focus on the issue at hand, people. I can assure you that the stalker would enjoy our little show here because he would hold all the trumps," the man warned them.

"You're right," Becka sighed. "Anyway, it's decided. Where Bryan goes, I follow," she narrowed her eyes and tilted her head, challenging her husband to contradict her.

"Right," Bryan tapped the tabletop with his hand. "Let's get back to business," he said, and waving his hand, the man invited his wife to sit down back in her chair.

"I say that Ariel should call the police first," Max proposed, glancing at the young woman, who nodded. "Do you have the police officers' number anywhere else but in your phone contacts?" he asked her.

"I have a business card in my bag," Ariel said and started rummaging through her bag.

It didn't take too long to find the card. Ariel was nothing else but an order freak, and everything had a particular spot in her handbag.

"Good," Max said. "Here's my mobile," he handed Ariel his phone. "Make the call to the police now. That way, we can push that out of the way," the man invited her after he entered his pin on the keyboard. "Maybe you'd better tell them that we're headed back to your house now," Max glanced up at Ariel. "We don't want to spend too much time there, and I don't think it would be a good idea to call them to my house," the man explained.

"You're right," Ariel nodded and started dialing the number that one of the officers had given her that day.

"When she finishes with the call, we should discuss the rest of the details," Max glanced at Becka and Bryan, who nodded in full agreement with him.

The call went through, and Ariel explained what happened. The people in the kitchen witnessed only her side of the conversation, but they understood that she had arranged to meet the police at her place.

"They can't come immediately," Ariel warned them. "The officer said that it will take about an hour until they get there," she explained, and her eyes reflected her fear.

"We are four people," Max reassured her. "We can manage. I'm confident that we can," the man looked at the others, and both Becka and Bryan nodded.

CHAPTER EIGHTEEN

Max persuaded them to go and take Ariel's phone from her place immediately. Thus, they had the time to check the voicemail the stalker had left for her before the police came.

Max had become somewhat mistrustful of the police at the news that the attacker was out on bail. Bryan had pointed out that it wasn't the police officers' fault that the guy got out, but Max hadn't wanted to listen to reason.

Anyway, everybody accepted his proposition. Becka and Bryan understood that they couldn't sway Max, and Ariel thought she would have time to pack some clothes. She couldn't spend a few days as Max's guest only in a pair of jeans and a pullover.

Ariel also insisted on taking her roller pin back home with her. However, the others looked at her as if the woman had lost her marbles.

"I didn't know that you were so keen on baking," Becka said in an astonished voice.

Except for aunt Marjorie, no one in their family liked to cook. Of course, if she didn't consider the people that had joined the family through marriage. Becka always stated that the cooking gene had skipped her clan.

"I don't bake," Ariel corrected her haughtily, considering that Becka's assumption diminished her. "However, the roller pin is mine. Besides, I think it is the best weapon in my arsenal," she explained to the other three people.

"Wouldn't it be your only weapon?" Max whispered in her ear, and Ariel grimaced, understanding the validity of the man's opinion.

"That's why it is the best," she pointed out, retrieving the rolling pin and starting toward the hallway to the front door. "Aren't you coming?" the young woman glanced back, a brow curved on her forehead.

The other three rushed after her, each of them trying to keep their amusement in check. Ariel was funny when she reacted both in character and out of it at the same time.

"Either she changed, or you cast a spell on her," Bryan told Max in an undertone.

Max snorted. The man shook his head and waved his hand dismissively.

"I don't think that anyone could change this woman," he whispered back to Bryan. "Ariel's got the stubbornness of a mule. She also has the bearing of a peacock, which is full of the importance of its plumage," Max added.

Ariel turned back to them in a fury.

"What the heck are you talking about?" she shouted at Max. "That's what you think of me?" the woman asked, and her tone of voice betrayed her hurt.

"I might not have expressed myself correctly," Max tried to soothe her down. "I meant to say that you don't take into consideration anyone's opinions and ideas but yours. I also consider that you think that you are above us, the common mortals," the man explained, looking straight into the woman's stormy green eyes.

Max didn't mean to hurt or offend Ariel. However, the woman had trampled all over his emotions a week before. She effectively crushed his feelings and hopes under the soles of her boots. Consequently, the man didn't believe that Ariel had the right to expect not to be judged for her narrow-mindedness.

His feelings for her hadn't disappeared just because Ariel didn't respond to them. However, the man didn't think that loving her meant not to see that the woman was riddled with flaws. That wasn't love. It was conscious blindness.

Ariel groaned, exasperated, and stomped out to the front door. There, she stopped, afraid of what might wait for her beyond the door.

Max noticed her hesitation and pushed her gently aside, opening the door and going out first. The man reached out to Ariel, who put her small hand in his and followed him.

Becka poked her husband, pointing her chin to the couple in front of them, and Bryan nodded. He wasn't very comfortable with the way things evolved, though.

The man had already surmised that Ariel was a material girl. He didn't expect that the woman would change her views because she experienced some feelings for Max. It was evident she did, but that didn't mean that the young woman would act on them.

Max proposed that they all piled up in his SUV and left the other cars in Bryan's garage. They embraced his idea and parked Ariel's car next to Bryan's.

Then, Max insisted on driving, despite Ariel's arguments against that. However, the man had already learned to deal with the pain in his arm for about a week. He knew he could do it.

Max won that battle and proved to Ariel that she was wrong. He could steer the wheel competently, even though a prong of pain still shouted through his arm now and then.

From her seat in the back of the car, Ariel watched Max from under her lashes. A lock of dark hair had fallen and covered half of the man's face, and the woman hardly contained herself not to reach to brush it away. She couldn't contradict her words with actions.

Besides, the others might have thought that she had lost her mind because of the stress she lived through. Ariel had never liked to be seen as a weakling.

Still, Ariel decided to profit from their temporary reunion and look at Max at her heart's content. Thus, she would memorize his features for later in life. If she was supposed to spend her life alone, then at least, she would have her fill right then.

When Max stopped the car on the driveway next to her house, Ariel's trepidation went up a notch. The woman didn't have a good feeling about their enterprise.

She glanced at her home with apprehension. Ariel didn't want to step inside the house. The woman shook her head to clear it. After all, she had loved that house for years, and she'd never felt something like that since she bought it.

Ariel got out of the car but didn't advance toward the steps leading to the front door.

"Don't be afraid," Max whispered in her ear, cradling her elbow in his hand. "I'm here. And Becka and Bryan are here too. You're not alone," the man insisted in a persuasive murmur.

Ariel nodded, albeit with hesitation, and she allowed the man to lead her to the front door of her house.

"Give me the key, Ariel," Max asked her.

Ariel moved the rolling pin under her arm and fished the key from her handbag. Then she handed it to Max. Briefly, she stole a glance at the man's eyes, but she turned her eyes down immediately. That face tore through her resolve, and the woman didn't like it.

CHAPTER NINETEEN

"Give me your keys," Max demanded to Ariel, stretching his hand.

The woman handed him her keys, and the man unlocked the front door. He pushed the door open and waited for a second, listening intently to possible noises coming from the interior.

Ariel had forgotten to leave the light on in her rush to flee the house. The entry hallway was dark, and the woman trembled almost imperceptibly.

Max patted her arm and went inside first. His gesture encouraged Ariel, and the woman followed him immediately.

Suddenly, the door closed behind her with a bang. It hit Bryan, who was coming after her, right in the face with force. The man fell backward, tripping over his wife, who cried out in distress but couldn't stop his fall.

Both ended in a pile at the foot of the stairs. Bryan remained still on the concrete alley, knocked out because of the savage hit in the face.

Becka was conscious, but she didn't fare much better than her husband. The man's weight over her body knocked the wind out of her. The woman gasped for a couple of minutes. She tried to pull air into her lungs and to untangle her body from underneath Bryan.

When she managed to get out from under him, Becka plopped down for a few moments, breathing hard. Everything hurt, but the woman didn't think that she broke anything.

Becka recovered soon, and then she leaned over her husband, fearing that he might have had a concussion. The man hadn't stirred for a second, although she perceived his shallow breathing.

"Come on, Bryan, open your eyes," Becka slapped him gently over the face, and accents of panic tainted her voice.

The woman threw a glance at Ariel's front door, but then she shook her head. For the moment, she needed to see what she could do with Bryan. The woman hoped that Max would take good care of Ariel because Becka wouldn't have forgiven herself if her sister got hurt while she tended to her husband.

Becka attempted to shake Bryan, but the man was too massive for her to have any success in her endeavor. Tears began streaming down her face, and the woman implored her husband to get back to the real world. Now, she was afraid that Bryan might have been seriously hurt and needed to go to the hospital.

***

On the other side of the closed door, a blow to the head threw Max into one of the walls. The man fell to the tiled floor. He groaned and shook his head to take his bearings.

Max felt dizzy, and the fog in his brain didn't help him too much. Still, the pain that ran through his wounded arm didn't allow him to lose consciousness, and he was grateful for that.

The man wondered what happened to Ariel, and the thought that the woman might be in grave danger helped him stand up.

The darkness in the hallway didn't matter to him right then because he couldn't focus his sight anyway. Max listened intently for the slightest noise but didn't hear a thing.

Suddenly, some rustling came from his right, and then Ariel's pitched scream stabbed him in the heart.

Max fisted his hands and bared his teeth. He should have protected the woman. Instead, he had fallen under the first blow to his chin.

The man hurried toward the source of the clamor and found himself in the living room. A stray ray from the lamppost outside tamed the obscurity of the room, and Max could see a man fighting with Ariel. The image prompted his blood to run cold.

The guy had lodged his fingers into Ariel's hair, pulling her head back. At the same time, he fought her, trying to take the roller pin from her hand.

Judging the man's face, Ariel had already succeeded in striking him with it. The man might have deflected most of the blow, but the side of his face and chin wore traces of blood, and the sign of a future bruise had appeared on his left cheekbone.

Max rushed to aid the young woman. Exactly when he pulled the man toward him, this one managed to dislodge the rolling pin from the woman's hand, twisting her wrist in the process. Ariel screamed in pain, and Max saw red before his eyes.

The attacker threw the pin right through the French door into the garden. His strength astounded and terrified Ariel, who froze on the spot.

Max didn't bother to look in the direction of the pin, even though he heard the clatter of broken glass. He pulled the intruder toward him and away from Ariel, and he planted his fist into his mouth.

Spit and blood flew out of the man's mouth, and an angry cry filled the room. The man responded in kind, and the ferocity of the blow pushed Max back a few steps.

"Run out of here," he yelled at Ariel while trying to regain his balance.

The man had noticed that the woman's glassy eyes stared at them, and he understood that she was under shock.

"Get out of here, Ariel," he shouted more forcefully, and this time the woman shook her head to clear it and looked at him. "Out, now," Max yelled again, and then he countered the fist, aiming at his face.

The invader was a massive man, and he could pack a lot of force in his blows. Besides that, Max discovered that the man had had some training in fighting and that training went beyond basic.

Max was good at what he did for a living, but he knew that weight played a decisive role in fights. That was why fighters didn't fight people from different weight classes.

Still, Max counted on his experience. He had gained it not only on the mat but also during his rescue missions around the world, so he did have an advantage.

Max also knew that his left arm wouldn't help him much, and he hoped the stalker wouldn't remember how severely he had been hurt. Otherwise, the man would take advantage of Max's weakness.

The two men exchanged quick blows and kicks, and both got bloody in no time. Grunts came from both sides, and both men seemed to be in a sea of pain.

Mesmerized, Ariel watched the fight from the door. At the first groan, the young woman couldn't step any farther, and she stopped there. She kept pressing her hands on her stomach, afraid that she would throw up soon.

Ariel had never seen such savage pounding, and she didn't understand how the men could still stand up. On the back of her mind, the thought that she should do something and end everything kept popping up, but the woman couldn't think of anything beyond that.

Max's left arm had started bleeding where the stitches gave way, and Ariel shook her head in denial. Tears began wetting her cheeks, and she leaned on the jamb of the door, suddenly feeling weaker than before.

The intruder threw Max on the floor and stepped toward him to finish the job. Max shook his head, trying to get a clear image of the man through the fog that insisted on covering his sight.

He wiped out the sweat on his forehead with the back of his hand and brushed his hair back. The thought that he should have bound it crossed his mind, but he chased it away immediately. It wasn't worth pondering on that right then.

Max instinctively knew that he had to stand up and jumped to his feet. The man approached him, and Max countered the man's blow with a high kick.

With a groan, the attacker landed at a short distance from the riff-raff of the coffee table. They had already broken that when Max fell over it earlier. He still felt the aches of the bruises he had acquired then.

Extenuated, Max didn't attack, knowing that the man needed at least a few seconds to get his wind back. He preferred to pull some air into his lungs first. It hurt when he breathed, a sign that at least one of his ribs was bruised, if not broken.

Then Max headed toward the man on the floor to finish the job. However, this one swiftly took out a knife he kept in one of his boots, and Max's eyes widened. The weapon changed the odds and dramatically.

An ugly grin turned up on the stalker's lips, and Max glanced at the door, where he'd seen Ariel earlier.

"Now go," he ordered to her quietly. "I'm not kidding," Max frowned at her.

Ariel made a few steps back, ready to run out of the room, but Max couldn't wait to see what the woman would do. The knife slashed to his face, and the man barely had the time to jump back.

Unfortunately, Max tripped over the edge of the round carpet in the middle of the room and fell. The massive attacker jumped over him and knocked the air out of his lungs. Still, when the knife made a move to his chest, Max deflected it, and the man stabbed his shoulder.

Max felt like fainting, and nausea hit his throat. Despite his sorry state, the man wriggled, trying to get out from under his enemy.

When with a shout, the assailant pulled the knife out of Max's arm, Max screamed in agonizing pain. The man raised the blade over his head, determined to shove it into his victim's chest.

Then he decided to make sure that Max wouldn't wriggle out of the way. He moved one of his knees over Max's left arm, prompting him to shout in pain once more.

Max closed his eyes, his brain descending into darkness. The aggressor immobilized his other arm with his left hand, leaning forward, to apply more pressure on the figure prone to the floor.

Ariel's distressed cry aroused Max from his temporary blackout, and he opened his eyes. The man knew he should do something, but he couldn't move his arms. Max tried to kick with his feet but didn't have too much success.

With remorse and regret, Max tried to glance at Ariel one last time. When his gaze fell on the woman, his breath hitched. The green of her eyes became incandescent, hurting his sight. Her lips parted, and the woman stretched her right arm in front of her and spread her fingers.

The knife flew from the attacker's hand, and the man cried out in disbelief. Max's eyes rounded, and the man licked his dry lips. He was convinced that he had lost too much blood and now hallucinated.

Swiftly, the knife landed in the woman's hand. Ariel shoved her other hand in front of her, and suddenly, Max didn't feel the man's weight on him any longer. A heavy thump announced that something had hit the wall at high velocity.

With a tremendous effort, he raised his torso. Max saw that the man had landed on the other side of the room after bouncing off the wall. Max's gaze zeroed on a crack in the wall. He could have sworn that it hadn't been there before.

When Ariel brushed her fingers on the side of his face, Max turned his gaze at her. He still couldn't believe that the woman was responsible for all that.

"Yes, that was my secret," Ariel nodded, reading his thoughts accurately. "Although, I didn't think I would ever be able to do something like that," she grimaced. "I'm sure you'd like to run away from me like lightning right now," the woman added, and sadness filled her voice.

"Are you out of your mind?" Max asked her in an incredulous tone of voice. "That was awesome. I always believed that it was a grain of truth in those comics I've always liked to read," the man said and then closed his eyes. "I think I'll just lie here for a while, Ariel. I see that you don't need me to protect you," he murmured, sliding into unconsciousness.

"That's where you're wrong," the woman murmured, gently touching the man's bruised face, and then she sat down next to him. "I need you to protect me from myself," Ariel murmured. So, don't you dare to die on me," she warned the man.

The woman took his hand in hers and rhythmically breathed in and out to get rid of her anxiety. She knew that what she had done meant only one thing, and she needed to come to terms with that.

'At least I got my powers,' she shrugged, pulling her knees up and leaning her head on top of them.

A few minutes later, the screech of brakes in her driveway made her lift her head. Ariel listened intently and then leaned over Max and said, "I think the police have arrived, Max. We'll take you to the hospital soon. Won't that be a fun trip?" she scrunched her nose.

The woman remembered well their last trip to the emergency room. She had hoped not to have the occasion to go through a second one.

"Yep, you were wrong, Ariel," the young woman murmured. "Another thing, I have been wrong about," she admitted with a shrug. "They keep popping up," she noticed with dismay.

CHAPTER TWENTY

The police car stopped in front of Ariel's house, and the police officers rushed out immediately. They had noticed the couple sitting at the feet of the staircase, and their position told them that things were not good at all.

Bryan had regained his consciousness but couldn't get up without getting sick and dizzy. Seeing that bruises covered both Becka and Bryan, the officers called for an ambulance.

"What happened?" one of them asked Becka. Bryan didn't seem able to answer any questions yet.

"We were about to get into the house," Becka pointed to Ariel's front door. "Max, our friend, went inside first. Ariel followed," the woman swallowed hard and started massaging her throat. She was trying not to cry, and the effort put pressure on her vocal cords.

"And then?" the officer prompted her, seeing that she stopped.

"Then the door was shut with force and hit my husband in the face. Bryan fell backward, his inertia taking me with him," Becka explained, waving her hand restlessly. "He lost consciousness for a while," she added, touching Bryan's forehead with the tip of her fingers. "It took me a little while to get out from under him," the woman said, pressing her lips for a few moments. "He's not a small man, as you can see," she pointed toward her husband's body.

"I understand," the police officer nodded sympathetically. "What about the other two people who got inside?" he wanted to know.

Becka shook her head and then burst into tears. She tried to control herself, but instead, she began sobbing uncontrollably. The woman felt guilty that she hadn't attempted to help her sister, even though she knew that Ariel had Max inside with her.

The police officer looked away from the young woman. He didn't know how to make her stop crying.

Bryan seemed to recover a bit more and slid his arm around the woman's shoulders, pulling her to his chest.

"My sister in law and my friend are inside," Bryan explained to the officer. "I suppose someone should go and see what happened there. I have heard some things, but I was out most of the time," the man said apologetically. "That door caught me right between the eyes and knocked me out for a while. I think I've got a concussion," Bryan touched the dark purple bump on his forehead with his fingers and groaned.

"No problem, sir," the officer patted the man's arm. "We'll see to it, and an ambulance is on its way here," he assured Bryan. "They should take care of you in no time."

"I imagine the ones inside might need more care than I do," Bryan responded in a grim tone of voice, afraid of what might lay behind that closed door.

"We'll see, and if it's necessary, we'll call another ambulance," the officer replied.

Then, the man rose and joined his colleague near the police car.

"We have to go inside," he told the other officer. "The woman is inside together with a man and the stalker," he informed his younger colleague. "We don't know what to expect, so you must be careful," the man warned the other.

With a nod, the young man followed the officer to the front door. They tried to open the door, but it appeared to be stuck or locked. However, the older officer was inclined to believe that the second alternative seemed more possible.

The older officer pointed his chin toward Bryan, who still sat at the foot of the staircase, and said, "Considering what that guy told us, "we must break the door and go in. The two people inside might be in distress," the man pointed out.

The two officers joined forces and rammed into Ariel's front door. Startled, Bryan and Becka looked up when the wood gave away, and the police officers stumbled into the house. Bryan gathered his wife closer to his chest and brushed his chin over the top of her head.

"I think everything will be fine," he reassured her, and Becka nodded hesitantly.

Inside, the officers advanced along the hallway toward the living room. They reached the door and leaned slightly forward to assess the interior. The silence seemed ominous, and they needed to progress carefully.

Ariel perceived motion from the corner of her eye and turned her head to the door. Her sight had already been accustomed to the darkness, so she realized immediately that the two figures were police officers.

"You can come in, officers," the woman invited them in an exhausted tone of voice. "It seems that I am the only one standing, metaphorically speaking," she said with bitterness. "The switch is on the wall on the right," Ariel advised them, tilting her head in that direction.

Only afterwards, the woman realized that they couldn't see her. The moon had hid behind a cloud, and the light had already disappeared.

However, the older officer reached out and turned on the light. He blinked when the darkness went away and then tried to adjust his eyes to the new environment. The man swept the room with his eyes, and surprise covered his features.

The man turned to his young colleague and shook his head. Wide-eyed, the officer brushed his fingers over his chin. He had never had to see such a scene, and the sight unnerved him.

"Go and check that man there," the older officer nudged him, tilting his head toward Max, who lay next to Ariel. "I suppose that's the stalker, miss," he spoke to the woman, pointing to the prone silhouette on the other side of the room.

"Yes, he is," Ariel said but didn't offer any more information.

The woman still didn't know how to explain that the man had been knocked out. She could say that she had taken the knife from him after he fell down. However, Ariel hadn't concocted a story for the rest yet.

The policeman approached the man on the floor carefully. He kneeled, checked his vitals, and concluded that the guy was just knocked out. The officer slapped a pair of handcuffs on the aggressor and then looked over the man's bloody parts and bruises, shaking his head. The man had been beaten to a pulp.

The policeman returned to his colleague, who was looking over Max. Noticing the quantity of blood the man suffered, the officer swallowed hard. The thought that they might have a lot of problems because, previously, they hadn't taken the woman's complaints seriously crossed his mind.

"I think we need to call two more emergency crews," he said quietly. "Call it in," he asked his colleague, checking Max's pulse.

Suddenly, the siren of the first emergency services car filled the night, and the officer rose. "I'm going out to talk to the paramedics. I think they should take this guy first. The guy outside is in a relatively good state. You remain here with them," he ordered to his younger colleague.

Startled, Ariel's raised her head. "Are Becka and Bryan fine?"

"Yes, miss, don't worry. They have a few bruises from falling down the stairs. It's possible that the man has a concussion, but only the EMT can determine it," he threw over the shoulder on his way out.

Relieved, Ariel sighed deeply, and a tear trailed down her cheek. At least, she wasn't responsible for any grave health problems that might have plagued Becka and Bryan.

***

Max left in the first ambulance, and Ariel went with him. The woman had declared herself Max's fiancée, and she had turned everything into a dramatic scene only to be allowed to ride with him. The older police officer implored the EMT experts to take her so that she would stop carrying on like a deranged lunatic.

Max came to the real world in the middle of Ariel's performance for a few moments, and the woman's statement shocked him into silence. He couldn't believe that he had before his eyes the same woman that had rejected him mercilessly less than a week before.

"Let her come," he managed to whisper, but he needn't have troubled himself.

No one heard his words, and anyway, the woman proved to have enough stamina to win that battle by herself.

All the way to the emergency care, Ariel held Max's hand and caressed his face and hair as gently as possible. The man watched her gestures with befuddlement. Nevertheless, in the end, convinced that he hallucinated, Max closed his eyes and surrendered to the fantasy.

At the hospital, he wanted to take control of his care and make sure that no one could take advantage of his condition. The man tried to get rid of everyone, but his weakened state helped everyone walk roughshod over him.

Luckily, Ariel from his fantasy world seemed to also have the power to order people around and make sure that they gave him the attention he needed. She also warned them not to poke or prod at him without a specific purpose.

Despite his aches and wounds, a satisfied grin perched on the man's lips, and he stopped fighting the people who helped him.

"I have my angel to take care of me," Max told everyone in a quiet tone of voice, which took everyone by surprise. Then, the man flexed his fingers over Ariel's to convey his gratitude.

For a second there, Ariel stared at him with puzzlement. Then, the woman burst into laughter and tears at the same time, and shaking her head in disbelief, she said, "Oh, you sweat, crazy, dear man."

The man didn't enjoy the medical care too much, but he listened to Ariel's encouraging words and soldered through it. When they finally put him in a private room, Max sighed with relief and thanked Ariel for all her help.

"You don't have to thank me," the woman replied, brushing his hair away off his forehead. "You're here because of me," she whispered, and then she tenderly touched his lips with hers.

Afraid that he wouldn't have the chance to experience anything of the kind, Max closed his eyes to enjoy that sign of affection at maximum. His thoughts mingled, and the confusion overwhelmed him.

When Ariel raised her head and smiled at him, Max reached out and took her hand. He laced his fingers with hers, squeezed them gently, and then said, "I'm here because of you, Ariel. If it hadn't been for you, I'd lay dead on that stupid carpet in your living room," the man explained to her.

"You know I wasn't talking about that," Ariel tried to stand up, but Max pulled her hand.

His strength wasn't what it used to be, and the woman could have broken free. However, she chose to remain where she was.

"Don't be stupid," the man retorted, upset. "We both know that that idiot who stalked you started everything. You can't think that you're somehow guilty."

"I know, but everything happened because of me," Ariel said with sadness in her voice.

"You can't take responsibility for another's person's actions," Max shook his head warily. "Anyway, you've got rid of him for good, so let's talk about more interesting things," he proposed with a grin on his lips.

"Yeah, we should," the woman agreed, and the far-away look in her eyes told the man that she was lost in her thoughts.

"What's the problem?" he inquired quietly, pulling her hand to make her pay attention to him.

Ariel glanced at him from under her lashes. "You do realize that the police will want to know what happened at my house."

"Ah, I see," Max nodded gingerly, afraid that his headache would get worse. "I suppose they will ask what happened, but we don't need to tell them the truth. They wouldn't believe it anyway," he pursed his lips, pondering the matter.

Ariel sighed and then asked, "What are you thinking about?"

"Let's tell them that I managed to kick the stalker in the chest with my foot. I suppose that's where your blow landed," he said in an inquiring tone of voice.

"More or less," Ariel fidgeted under his scrutiny. "I aimed for the chest and forehead instinctively. Probably, at a subconscious level, I thought that a double blow would do the trick," she explained.

"All right then," Max said and started analyzing the possibilities. "This might be a bit of a stretch, but we can say that I used a double kick in rapid succession, and the effort knocked me down for good. I can't see how else the guy could have been hit both in the chest and forehead," he explained apologetically.

"Do you think it would work?" Ariel worried.

"It's two of us," Max pointed out. "If both of us stick with the story, they can't prove us wrong. Besides, as I've already said, no one would believe that you knocked the man down," he reiterated.

Ariel nodded, although she wasn't very convinced that their explanation would stand scrutiny.

"By the way, how did you do it?" Max asked her with curiosity in his voice.

"ESP," Ariel replied dryly. "At a certain level, I knew that I had the gift, but I wasn't aware that I reached the point where I could use it," she said, and a derisive smile curved her lips. "It really shocked me, Max," she told him in earnest. "I was convinced that my gifts would never amount to anything," the young woman shook her head with sadness.

"Why?" the man asked.

"Well…," the woman started to explain when the door opened.

Ariel turned her head to the door in time to see the head of the older police officer, who was looking inside the hospital room.

"Sorry to bother," the man apologized. "The doctor said that we could pass by and ask a few questions."

"Come in," Ariel invited them, after glancing at Max and seeing his nod of approval.

"We won't keep you long," the officer promised. "I know you've been through a lot tonight."

"Thank you, we appreciate it," Max replied.

"We already know how everything started. Your sister and her husband told us," the man said to Ariel. "However, we don't really know what happened inside, and what the aggressor is saying doesn't make any sense," he explained.

"What is he saying?" Max inquired with a hint of curiosity in his voice, although the man could imagine what the guy was saying.

"He's saying that she had thrown him into the wall by charging him with a beam of power," exclaimed the younger police officer in a voice filled with exhilaration, pointing toward Ariel.

His colleague rolled his eyes and shook his head. "I've already told you that the guy is mad like a hatter. The ER doctor even asked for an assessment in the psychiatric ward," the man turned back to Ariel and Max.

"That sounds like a good idea," Max approved, thinking that the stalker had some screws unscrewed anyway and could use a good psychiatrist.

"So what happened?" the officer asked them.

"I can't give you an account blow by blow," Max replied. "I can tell you that he hit me first when I got into the house. I blacked out for a few moments, and when I came back, I found him fighting with Ariel and trying to pull the roller pin from her hand," the man said.

"Oh, yes, I forgot about my roller pin," Ariel said with a sad smile on her lips.

"Hey, it helped," Max consoled her. "If you hadn't had that roller pin, the man could have done anything to you until I regained my consciousness," he explained.

"Probably you are right," Ariel shrugged. Right then, she couldn't be bothered to think about what might have happened.

"What next?" the officer insisted. He didn't have time to go through what might have happened. The man wanted to write his report and go home. After all, he had already cumulated several hours of overtime that day.

"I lit into him," Max said. "I hit him, and he hit me. We fell a few times. I remember that I fell over the coffee table once," the man shrugged. "I'm sorry, Ariel. I think you'll need a new one," he apologized.

"Don't worry about it," the woman said. "I would have thrown it away anyway, as I will throw that damn carpet," she said heatedly with a frown.

"The carpet? Why?" the younger officer asked.

"Why? Because Max tripped over it and fell. That's when the stalker came to him with the knife and stabbed him," the woman explained angrily.

"How did you come out of that situation, sir?" the older police officer inquired, watching the man in awe.

"Honestly, I really don't know," Max said with remorse.

In reality, the man hadn't thought about that part of the story. He hadn't had the time to put together a credible response. Now, he had to wing it and hope that the officers would believe him.

"I only remember that I was thinking that I was done and Ariel would be left alone. However, somewhat I managed to untangle myself from underneath the man and got to my feet. With the last drop of strength, I kicked him twice and then fell to the floor. I can't remember too much after that," the man shook his head. "I think I told you to go and take the knife from his hand," he said to Ariel, raising his brows on his forehead.

"Yes, you did tell me that before you passed out," Ariel nodded. "Of course, I immediately ran to him and took the weapon," she said to the policemen. "I was afraid that the man would come out of his blackout. At least, thus, he wouldn't have had that cursed blade to attack us," the woman opened her arms to give more credibility to her story.

"Yes, of course," the older policeman approved her train of thought. "I think that's everything we needed. You don't have to worry anymore, miss," the man told Ariel. "He can't get bail again. Even if it turns out that he is not sane, the man still won't go out in the world a free man," he assured her.

"I hope so," the woman said matter-of-factly. "We've gone through a lot because of him and because you didn't believe me from the beginning," she continued with a deep frown.

"I know, miss, and I'm very sorry," the policeman repeated, and with a sign to his younger colleague, he took his leave.

On the way to the door, the younger officer whispered to his colleague, "Still, it would have been great if the woman did blast the man with that beam he was talking about."

His colleague shook his head exasperated and pushed him out of the door. Behind them, Max chuckled.

"What?" Ariel asked, glancing back at him.

"Oh, to be so young," the man grinned and tossed his head.

"Thank God, the other one is not so young anymore," Ariel noticed dryly.

"I hear you," Max nodded. "And you are right. Let's keep it a secret between us, sweetheart," he proposed, lacing his fingers with her.

"And my entire family," the woman scrunched her nose.

"Yes, you'll have to tell me a few things about that," Max observed.

"But not right now," Ariel contradicted him. "Let's focus on getting you back home soon."

"I couldn't agree more," the man's eyes darkened, despite the fever that shone in them. "Tell the doctor that I feel I'm fine enough to leave."

"Not this time," Ariel shook her head. "You must remain in here for at least a day or two."

"Are you out of your mind?" the man shouted and tried to jump out of bed, only to groan in pain.

"Calm down, you idiot," the woman pushed him back as tenderly as she could. "You can't go anywhere in the state you are. It's not just your arm this time, Max. You've got stabbed in the shoulder and kicked everywhere else," she pointed out. "Plus, you blacked out at least twice if not three times."

"I will survive," the man said stubbornly, a grim look on his face.

"That I guarantee," Ariel retorted in a decisive tone of voice. "That's because I will stay guard right here and won't let you move," she warned him.

"Really? You'll stay with me," Max repeated with disbelief.

"Yes, really," Ariel answered. "Now shut up. I need to call Becka and Bryan and see if they're all right," the woman ordered to Max.

The man shook his head but kept his mouth shut so that Ariel could make her call. He watched her talk, and a grin spilled on his face.

The man hadn't known that happiness would come to him that way when he lay in a hospital bed. His heart filled with joy while he watched the woman he held dear to his heart, asking questions and giving evasive answers. Ariel did walk a tight rope in her variant of the story. That amused Max a lot. .

CHAPTER TWNETY-ONE

Three weeks later, Ariel and Max visited Becka and Bryan. It was the first time Max had been allowed to go out of the house after his discharge from the hospital, and the man planned to enjoy himself.

Ariel had kept her promise and didn't move from his side during his first twenty-four hours in the hospital. Max even had to call a friend to bring her some food because she refused to go out and buy something for herself.

The young woman had also spent time with him at his place, and she almost moved in with him.

Ariel had arranged to have her house cleaned and asked to have the carpet and what was left of the coffee table thrown away, but she still didn't feel comfortable sleeping under that roof.

Ariel took good care of Max, and the man was grateful to her. Having her with him in his home was a dream come true.

However, the woman evaded most of his questions about the secret of her gifts. She only told him that she'd been insecure about her abilities because of an old curse but didn't go into details.

She was very good at avoiding some subjects, and Max hadn't found out more than what she had already told him in the hospital.

Still, the man consoled himself that Ariel would tell him everything when the time would be right. He needed to lie to himself because that status-quo drove him crazy.

That day, Max decided to relax with Ariel and his friends. Bryan surprised him with his favorite pastries, and for the first time, Max got to spend time with their kids.

The man had seen Lea and Sean before but for only a few minutes at a time. Either Becka or Bryan always found an excuse not to leave the children in his presence too long.

Max hadn't thought of that before, but that realization angered him.

"How come you allow me in the presence of your kids now?" he suddenly asked, with a frown.

"What are you talking about?" Becka asked, widening her eyes with innocence.

"Forget about charming me," Max pointed his finger to her. "I might be a bit slow, I know. It took me almost over a year to realize what is going on, after all. That doesn't mean that I'm entirely stupid," the man retorted, glancing furiously from Becka to Bryan and back.

"Break it out, Max," Ariel snapped at him. "They had to keep the children away from you because they also have their own gifts," she explained to him.

"Now you're talking," the man exclaimed with glee. "You have to explain to me how these things work. I understand that the children have gifts. Bryan kept them away from me so that I wouldn't find out about them. That's clear. That means that the kids can use their gifts. How come you couldn't use yours?" Max stared hard at Ariel.

"I've already told you that I couldn't use them because of a curse," the young woman retorted, throwing a withering glance at Max. "I don't really know why the kids can," Ariel admitted. "We've made a lot of assumptions but didn't reach any conclusion," the woman shrugged. After all, it didn't really matter because later in life, the children wouldn't be able to do what they do now."

Max shook his head. "It doesn't work that way. I'm sure you have an explanation," he insisted.

"We think that Lea and Sean can use their gifts because they are young and don't filter their intentions consciously," Bryan intervened. "And the problem is not that Ariel couldn't do anything, but that she couldn't control what she did."

"Exactly," Becka chimed in as well. "I was also in the same situation. I could do some things, but I couldn't control their magnitude or result, and that's dangerous. That's why Ariel stopped trying to do anything," Becka explained with a shrug.

"That makes sense," Max admitted. "What can you do?" Max asked Becka with curiosity, and lights danced in his eyes.

Ariel smiled and shook her head. The man behaved like a child in a candy store.

"What can't she do?" Bryan burst into laughter. "Storms, blizzards, things like that," he waved his hand in a circle to drive the point home.

"Oh, my gosh, that's something," Max shook his head in disbelief. "You can't cause storms, can you?" he turned to Ariel.

"No, I can't," the young woman smiled at him. "I can move objects and drive forces through things," she said. "What you've already seen," she pointed out. "And I can feel and read moods," the woman shrugged.

"That's cool anyway," Max patted her hand. "Besides, I don't know how comfortable I'd be if you started storms around the house," he wriggled his brows, jokingly.

All of them started laughing, and then Bryan offered some more drinks. Ariel felt relieved that the man took everything in stride. She didn't need the drama that usually came with such revelations.

"But what's that curse, Ariel?" Max didn't forget about his questions. "Who cursed you, and how the curse works?" the man wanted to know.

Ariel's eyes rounded, and the woman looked at him with anxiety.

"What's the problem, sweetheart?" Max grasped her hand, pulling the woman closer to him.

Ariel looked at Becka, mutely asking her sister to help her.

"I'll tell you," Becka told Max. "Ariel seems a little embarrassed, although I don't know why. It's just the way things work, Ariel," Becka shook her head.

"Still…" Ariel murmured and shook her head to her sister.

"Don't worry, I will explain," Becka assured her and then turned to Max. "Look, Max. Briefly, the situation is like this. Great-grandfather left Rebecca, our great-grandmother, for another woman. Of course, grandma got pissed off," Becka waved her hand in the air, and Bryan chuckled. "Anyway, afterward, Evelyne, my great-grandaunt, got left at the altar and committed suicide. Rebecca got so angry that she cursed all generations to come. No one wouldn't control and refine their abilities if they didn't find true love and committed to that person. That's all," Becka shrugged.

"Now I understand why you were so sure that you hadn't been in love with that guy," Max turned to Ariel. "You'd have had your powers if you'd loved him."

"Yes," Ariel admitted.

"So that means…" Max started to say but stopped, and closing his eyes, began to turn ideas around his mind.

He had a clear idea of what had happened but didn't want to jump the gun there. For his own sanity, he needed to be correct in his assumptions.

"You love me," he exploded after a couple of minutes, jumping off the sofa.

Becka and Bryan fought to contain their laughter, and Ariel's face got so red that they feared she would self-combust in an instant.

The young woman couldn't look at Max. Embarrassed, she stubbornly stared at the coffee cup that she had almost spilled when Max made his announcement.

"Come on, baby," he implored her. "You can simply nod if you think it would be easier than talking."

Bryan shook his head and said, "Max, sometimes you lack any kind of sensibility. You see that Ariel is embarrassed. Leave her be," he ordered to his friend.

"Why are you embarrassed?" Max insisted. "Are you ashamed of your feelings for me?" the man frowned, suddenly not very comfortable with that conversation.

Ariel swiftly turned her eyes to him. "Don't be stupid, Max. Of course, I'm not ashamed of my feelings. Still, after everything I told you that first day at your house, I don't feel quite happy with this discussion. Plus, this is something we should discuss alone, not in a group," she tilted her head toward Becka and Bryan.

The two of them vehemently nodded their agreement with her words.

"All right, I understand," Max put his hands up. "You are correct. We should talk about all this in private," he agreed with her. "But don't forget that you love me, and I love you," he stressed out, and Becka had to bite her lower lip not to start laughing again.

Ariel scrunched her nose, realizing that it was a waste of time to try and reason with the man. Max was blunt most of the time. If she wanted him, then she had to live with that.

"Good," Bryan remarked. "I'm happy that we've put this subject at rest," the man said dryly. "Maybe now we can try other avenues of discussion," he proposed.

"I'm all for it," Max nodded, taking his coffee cup from the coffee table in front of the sofa and sipping some of the black, potent liquid.

"Yes, how about that?" Ariel murmured with sarcasm, and Max looked at her sideways.

Then the man chuckled and shook his head. "No matter what you believe, Ariel, we do make a good team," he pointed out.

"Keep that thought in mind," Becka snorted.

She hadn't forgotten how willful her sister was. She also remembered that Bryan had mentioned Max's stubbornness several times. The two of them would fight like cats and dogs day in and day out. Still, Becka was happy that Ariel had found someone. She deserved to be happy and forget about lost opportunities.

Besides, Becka hoped that love might mollify Ariel somewhat, and it would be easier to live with her.

"Anyway, Ariel, don't forget," Bryan chimed in. "You also have to give Max the second part of the story. He might not like it if he heard it from someone else," he warned the young woman.

"What part of the story?" Max wanted to know.

"Later, when we are alone," Ariel replied in a tone of voice that didn't broach any argument.

The man grimaced but decided to respect her wishes for the moment. He wouldn't let her avoid that subject forever.

Not five minutes later, the kids woke up, and they all moved to the kitchen to have a snack with them. That involved a lot of laughter, and this time, Becka was the one who blushed most of the time.

Max wouldn't have traded that snack time for anything. The twins amused him with their ploys to outwit their parents, and Ariel seemed to relax more and more. Even Becka and Bryan had a hard time believing that she was the same woman who imparted lots of diminishing judgments and bitterness.

CHAPTER TWENTY-TWO

Bryan had just proposed to go back into the living room when the bell rang. The four adults looked on to another surprised, but the toddlers cheered, happy to have a new audience for their antics.

"Has anyone called to say that they would come to visit?" Bryan asked Becka, heading to the living room door.

"No," the woman shook her head. "Mom called earlier, but I told her that we were going to have guests, and she said she would come tomorrow then," Becka replied.

"All right," Bryan nodded and got out into the hallway to open the front door.

The man looked through the peephole to see who was ringing the bell impatiently. He inwardly groaned when his gaze fell on Rebecca.

He opened the door and greeted the older woman, "Hello, Rebecca. How come you are in our neighborhood?" Bryan raised his brows inquiringly, and an unsettling feeling churned his stomach.

He had a good idea why Rebecca showed at their door and where to place the guilt for that visit. Becka's mother never knew when to keep her mouth shut. Emilie must have thought that her intervention would help her daughter. That despite what she had witnessed the last few times when Rebecca had met the significant others in her grandchildren's lives. None of those meetings had gone well.

"Do you intend to keep me waiting here on the steps, young man?" the woman snapped at him, a deep frown set between her brows.

"No, by all means, come in. Still, keep in mind that the kids are also in the living room, and I don't want any dramatic outbursts," the man warned her in an authoritative tone of voice.

"Huh! These days, everyone thinks that they can tell me what I should do," the woman retorted sarcastically.

"When my children are in the middle, you can bet your life that I would tell you what I expect from you," Bryan didn't step back.

The woman snorted and pushed by him. "Won't you take my coat?" she raised a brow inquiringly.

The man sighed and reached out to help her take her winter coat off. He hung it in the hall wardrobe and then invited the older woman to the living room.

"Look what the cat dragged in," Bryan sarcastically said when they got there.

Becka's mouth opened, but no sound came out. Ariel groaned with dismay, and a grim grin perched on Max's lips. The man had a good guess why the woman had made that sudden appearance.

Only the children welcomed their great-grandmother with squeals of glee and ran to her.

"Now, easy there, children," the woman braced herself for their attack. "I don't want you to topple me down," she warned them sternly.

However, the woman kissed their cheeks and patted their heads. Then she rummaged through her voluminous handbag. After a thorough search, Rebecca took out a small chocolate bar and a tiny teddy bear for each of them.

Becka started toward them to protest about the chocolate, but Bryan waved her back and shook his head. He didn't think that a small bar would make a lot of difference and didn't want to start an argument with Rebecca about it.

The man knew that a quarrel was brewing anyway. He didn't want to pour more fuel on that specific fire.

"Now, go and play," Rebecca ordered the kids, with a pat on their behinds.

Sean looked at his toy and snorted. They didn't need useless things. However, the boy noticed his father's warning gaze and held his tongue.

"Won't you take a seat, grandma?" Becka waved toward an armchair that was far enough from Ariel and Max. "Bryan will bring you some coffee," she offered.

"Yes, I think I need to sit down for this discussion, but I won't need coffee," the older woman frowned. "I am so disappointed right now that I can hardly stand," she added, marching with heavy steps toward the armchair that Becka had shown her.

Bryan left the room and went to the kitchen to bring some coffee to the woman even if she had refused it.

Ariel watched her grandma from under her lashes. She remembered well what the woman had done to others. So, Ariel expected that the old woman would start spewing her venom soon.

Max looked unconcerned with the woman's presence. As long as Ariel stood by him, he didn't care what anyone else would say.

"You let me down, young lady," Rebecca turned to Ariel with hard eyes. "I thought you were the smartest of this bunch," she shook her head with disappointment.

"What do you mean?" Becka frowned at Rebecca.

The older woman fluttered her fingers dismissively, but Becka didn't back down.

"I asked what you mean, grandma," she said with anger in her voice.

"I'm not talking to you, Becka," Rebecca snapped at her younger great-granddaughter.

"But when you said *the smartest of this bunch*, you clearly included me in your conversation," Becka retorted, and her eyes shone with repressed fury.

"Well, consider that you are excluded," Rebecca waved her hand. "I don't have anything against Bryan. He's a smart man. I'm talking about the others, so shut up," the woman ordered.

"Rebecca, you know that I don't appreciate it when you take this tone with my wife," Bryan, who had just returned with her coffee, scolded her quietly.

The man also tilted his head toward the children, warning the older woman to watch her mouth. He didn't want that they witness Rebecca's rudeness toward their mother.

"For God's sake, would you all stop interrupting me?" Rebecca turned her thunderous eyes at Bryan. "I won't be deterred from saying what I came to say," the woman tapped her knee with her hand.

"Let the lady speak," Max intervened. The man had met the woman before and knew that she wouldn't stop imparting her views only because someone else didn't like it.

"I don't need your support," the old woman slashed the man with a dark gaze. "Now, you girl, what the heck were you thinking, throwing your lot with this lowlife scumbag?" she scolded Ariel with a grimace on her thin lips.

"I beg your pardon?" Ariel retorted haughtily, rising to her feet.

"You heard me well, girl," Rebecca replied. "You had a chance to get better things," she shook her head. "You still have," the woman warned her great-granddaughter. "But only if you get back to your senses."

"I'm pretty sure I've just regained my reason," Ariel braced her hands on her hips. "I kept listening to you and trying to do what you wanted," the young woman shouted. "And for what? To spend a sterile life, waiting for you to feed me crumbles?" she stomped her foot.

"Way to go, girl," Rebecca noted with sarcasm. "Do you think a toddler's tantrum would make me change my mind?" she waved her hand with scorn.

Ariel's eyes turned a darker green, and sparks seemed to erupt between the two women. The temperature rose with a few degrees, and Max's brows hiked up his forehead.

The man didn't know what to expect from a heated confrontation between the two women, but he imagined that things might get even weirder. He also wondered about the wisdom of being caught between the two.

However, Max couldn't abandon the battlefield. He had no intention to give up his claim to Ariel's heart.

Bryan silently closed the distance between him and Becka. "Take the kids upstairs, Becka. They're better off there, I think," the man whispered to his wife.

"No, she needn't take them from here," Rebecca turned to them. "They should learn from an early age where stupidity can land you," the woman said.

"I think they have enough time to learn what's good for them or not," Bryan noted quietly. "Becka," he turned a meaningful gaze to his wife.

Becka nodded and asked the children to follow her.

"But I want to stay and see," Sean protested when his mother took his hand. The child's icy blue eyes, very similar to his father's, turned rebellious. Unruffled, Bryan stared at him, and the boy immediately followed his mother without further comments.

Rebecca steamed a few seconds, considering Bryan's refusal to allow his children to witness the quarrel a personal affront. Then, the woman's gaze returned to Ariel.

"Let's end this charade, Ariel. If you want my money, you'll get rid of that leech," she pointed toward Max, whose eyes widened at her words.

"I see only a leech in this room," Ariel retorted haughtily. "And that's you. You'd love to suck the light of life out of us. You don't give anything without conditions, and you delight in our misery," the younger woman explained when her great-grandma's eyes bulged out.

Rebecca spluttered a few moments at a loss of words. The woman couldn't believe that Ariel had dared to utter such things. The color in her cheeks turned a darker red, and something started pounding in her temples.

Bryan looked at the older woman carefully and came to her. "Are you all right, Rebecca?" the man asked solicitously, afraid that the woman might have a stroke soon.

Rebecca pushed him forcefully away and tore into Ariel. "You ungrateful, prissy, useless woman. I wanted to give you everything because the rest of the lot cut themselves out. And that's how you thank me?" she shouted.

Flames danced in the woman's dark eyes, and the contrast of their color with the snow-white of her hair became more noticeable.

Max couldn't take his eyes off her. The woman might have seemed frail at first sight, but she mesmerized him with the strength her posture and anger revealed.

Ariel snorted with derision. "As if I'd believe you," the young woman fluttered her hand. "I did for a while," she admitted. "But then, I was convinced that I wouldn't ever find love," Ariel explained.

"That's what you call love?" Rebecca slashed Max with a dark gaze. "A pretty face, tattoos, and the mind of a peacock?" she asked sarcastically.

"Hey there," Max intervened, considering that he had allowed the woman to disparage him enough. "Watch your language," the man exclaimed, offended to be judged that way.

"You shut up, scumbag," the old woman retorted, and then she turned to Ariel.

The younger woman's eyes had already narrowed to slits, and her hands had balled into fists. Still, Ariel managed to remain somewhat calm. She knew that, probably, what Rebecca was going to say would drive her over the net.

"Look at him, for God's sake," Rebecca shouted, waving her hand toward Max with utmost contempt. "Really? Really, Ariel? I hoped more from you, girl," the old woman shook her white-haired head with disappointment.

Ariel simply stared at her great-grandmother with fire in her gaze. The young woman pressed her lips together so that she wouldn't speak before Rebecca had finished what she had to say. She thought it would have been better to get over with everything in one go.

"To fall for the first pretty-faced birdbrain with an aura of a bad boy is plain stupid," Rebecca shook her head angrily. "I repeat, Ariel. You'll send him packing if you know what's good for you. And then, I'll review my fund trust to give you a good chunk as an advance," the woman tried to persuade Ariel and turn her to her way of thinking. "When you find a nice man from a good family, you'll get the rest," Rebecca spelled out her conditions.

"Have you finished?" Ariel asked the older woman in a glacial tone of voice.

"How dare you?" Rebecca retorted, and the frown between her brows became deeper.

"Well, considering what you've just said, I don't need to refrain myself from pointing out the obvious," Ariel shrugged with indifference, although she was boiling inside. "So, you think that you can dangle your money before my nose, and I come to you like a loyal dog," the young woman surmised Rebecca's speech with a shake of her head. "I have bad news for you then, grandma," Ariel pursed her lips. "I can live without your pathetic handouts. I have everything I need here," she came to stand next to Max and put her hand on the man's forearm."

"Do you dare to challenge me, girl?" Rebecca narrowed her eyes to slits.

Ariel tilted her head and seemed to ponder the question for a moment. "I think I do," she said, and her voice betrayed that even she was a little surprised with that outcome.

Rebecca shook her head in denial. She couldn't believe that Ariel, the one that had always played by the rules and never broken one, was capable of rejecting her demands.

"Now, if everything is settled, I think we'll go back home, Bryan," Ariel said, turning to her brother in law, a thin smile on her lips.

The sparring with her great-grandmother had exhausted her. The young woman imagined that she would probably also hear from her mother that evening. She didn't doubt that Rebecca would call and complain about her behavior. That thought tired her even more.

"You're not going anywhere, young lady, until you tell me that you'll forget about this one," Rebecca pointed to Max. "I understand hormones," she tried to show some sympathy. "I was young once," the old woman explained in a honeyed tone of voice without going into particulars. "But that doesn't mean to throw everything out of the window. You don't need to buy the whole cow to get the milk if you know what I mean," she smiled thinly at Ariel.

For a second, the three people in the room stared at the old woman in shock. Bryan opened his mouth to say something but changed his mind and shook his head with disbelief. The man didn't even fathom what he could have said.

Max raised his brows so high on his forehead that they disappeared under his thick mane completely. The man's gaze turned to the woman next to him, tilting his head with curiosity. He needed to know what she had to say about that.

They hadn't even become lovers, and the man didn't want to pressure Ariel into anything. He believed that she would give him a sign when the time was right, although he hoped that that sign would come soon. He didn't know how long he would resist not sharing the bedroom with her.

Ariel wetted her lips nervously and squeezed the man's hand. She wanted to reassure him of her intentions, but she also needed some of his strength right then.

Max had shown her so much patience and steadiness that sometimes Ariel felt ashamed for how she had treated him before. Now she realized that she had been on the way to turn into a younger version of Rebecca for the last few years, and she loathed herself because of that.

The man, standing next to her right then, had shown her how life could be if she left her bitterness behind. Ariel wasn't about to turn that chance down, only to get some of Rebecca's money.

The young woman's dream had always been to build a nursery and landscape business. She knew that she might not be able to do it if she turned her great-grandmother's proposition down.

Nonetheless, Ariel understood that she would get something much more precious if she turned down Rebecca's deal. Anyway, the young hoped that Max would allow her to experiment with his extensive grounds. That should be enough to quench her thirst to design and grow a stylish garden.

In reality, the man hadn't proposed to her, but she had no doubt that he would. Max had chased her for far too long to give up now. The man had almost given his life in exchange for hers.

Max had already shown her how he felt, and Ariel was confident that the words would follow. The woman didn't believe that she would want anything else more from a man.

"So? What are you waiting, Ariel?" the older woman asked impatiently.

She had the feeling that her grip over the younger woman was getting weaker, and she wanted to press her to choose. Rebecca knew that Ariel loved money more than anything. The older woman hoped that giving her great-granddaughter something now might change the tide in her favor.

"I am waiting to calm down enough so that I could answer you with a shred of respect, just because you are the older member of our family," the young woman said.

"Great," Bryan intervened brusquely. "Maybe until Ariel regains her composure, I can offer you a drink, Rebecca," he asked the older woman. His voice reeked with forced solicitude, eager to derail the dark light that started glimmering in the woman's pupils.

"I don't need a drink now," the woman barked at him and threw him a look that would have made a weaker man turn into a puddle on the floor.

However, the blond giant took it in stride and didn't quake in his boots. Not that Rebecca expected him to cower in front of her. She knew him better than that, after all.

"But I do," Bryan replied with a forced smile on his lips. "Maybe you too," he turned to Max, who nodded vigorously.

The man felt his throat parched. He couldn't be more grateful to Bryan for his insight.

"Just a second, Max and I will pour you one," Bryan headed to the concealed bar in the living room. When he passed by Max, he winked at him and slapped him heartily over the shoulder.

"I don't have time for this nonsense," Rebecca shouted behind him.

"Everyone has time for a drink when they make a courtesy visit," Bryan grinned, turning his head to her. "Considering that you took the time to come here, I'm sure your schedule is free this afternoon, Rebecca. Let's relax and have a nice visit," the man said after opening the bar.

He doubted that such a thing was possible, but talking nonsense sometimes helped. Bryan knew that they needed all the possible help right then. Rebecca was on the verge of exploding.

"And if you don't have the time, then we won't keep you any longer," Ariel chimed in with forced joy.

For a couple of seconds, Rebecca spluttered. The woman couldn't find her words. Then, the inferno broke free.

CHAPTER TWENTY THREE

Rebecca's face scrunched, and the woman took a few furious steps toward Ariel. Max immediately pulled the woman behind him and confronted the old woman.

"Don't you dare to put your hands on her," he warned Rebecca with a hard stare.

"I'll do much more than putting my hands on her," the woman replied in a harsh tone of voice. "Now move on, slug," she waved him aside.

"I don't think so," Max shook his head, not budging an inch, although Ariel was pushing him from behind so that she could get in the face of her great-grandmother.

Bryan put his hands up and headed toward the older woman. The man realized that the situation had just become worse than ever before, and he needed to disarm the tension.

"Rebecca, let's discuss things with calm and reason," the man proposed, gently touching the woman's arm.

Suddenly, Rebecca pushed her arm against him. Bryan flew away, and his flight stopped on the sofa. The man groaned when he landed on the cushions. Although they softened his landing, the air still got knocked out of his lungs.

Bryan stared at Rebecca with astonishment. He couldn't believe that the woman had physically attacked him, and he tried to regain his breath to berate the old witch.

The older woman glanced at him for a second. She wanted to make sure that the man wasn't hurt. She loved Bryan, after all. That didn't mean that she would accept his interference, though.

Rebecca was a woman with a purpose. She had already lost contact with most part of her great-grandchildren because of their stubbornness. The woman didn't want that the same thing happened with Ariel.

Wide-eyed, Max looked from Rebecca to Bryan and back. The woman's action had shocked him. The man had never really thought what entitled being a witch. Now that he saw the effects, Max started doubting his abilities to protect Ariel or himself in front of the woman.

"Move away right now, Max," Ariel punched him in the back. "The old bat wants me, not you," she shouted.

"Yeah, you're out of your mind, baby," the man scowled. "Probably the temperature rise affected your brain," he remarked, pushing her back.

Rebecca strode purposefully toward the two young people, and her demeanor terrified Max. Still, the man didn't budge and watched the old woman with hard eyes, doing his best to hide his fear.

The woman stopped less than a meter away. Her eyes shone with anger, and her face was covered with a red hue. The woman furiously pressed her lips in a thin line, and her chest was rising and falling under a heavy breath.

Bryan understood that Rebecca could do anything at that moment and tried to rise from the sofa. The man didn't know what he could do to stop the inevitable, but he couldn't remain there and watch his best friend's demise. He wasn't even sure that Ariel would fare better than Max.

Rebecca spread her fingers and pushed the air in front of her with her palms. At the same time, Bryan shouted her name from the top of his lungs. The old woman didn't seem to hear him, though. She pushed harder and to the right, and Max flew to the floor with a resonant thump.

The man groaned. Old aches came back to life, and blood trickled from the corner of his mouth. Max tried to support himself in his arms to stand up and felt a stabbing pain in his left arm. *'Damn it. I just got rid of stitches. Not again, damn it,'* he swore under his beard.

Ariel had frozen for a couple of moments, watching Max thrown away like a puppet. The young woman had also lost balance for a few seconds, but she managed to keep her legs under her.

The young woman rushed to Max and helped him rise off the floor. The man didn't look too well, and the gray of his face worried her.

Ariel turned toward Rebecca and spat through tight teeth, "You'll pay for that, you dark, crazy witch."

Rebecca smirked and raised her hands again, this time against Ariel.

"Becka," shouted Bryan at the end of his wits. "Come downstairs now!" he yelled as loud as possible while finally getting off the sofa and rushing toward Rebecca.

The older woman turned to him, and the obsidian of her eyes terrified Bryan. Unaltered fury shone in there, and he understood that the woman wouldn't listen to reason. The man thought of getting to Rebecca and mobilizing her, but the woman shoved against the air in front of him, and Bryan flew back from where he'd started.

Ariel put her palms up, and the green of her eyes darkened and became black. The young woman bared her teeth and pushed her palms forward, shouting an old Indian battle cry.

Max watched her astounded and scrambled to get to his feet.

Rebecca stumbled but regained her balance swiftly. With a cackle, the woman turned against her great-granddaughter and threw a bolt of lightning against her.

"No, you won't," Max yelled with all his might and threw himself between Rebecca and Ariel. The lightning speared him, and the man fell down.

Ariel froze for a moment, but then, forgetting about Rebecca, she rushed to Max. The young woman touched his lips with her palm and waited to feel his breath on her skin. She placed the other palm on the man's chest and pressed forcefully against it.

Victorious, Rebecca laughed and got ready to strike Ariel. There was no one there to protect the young woman anymore.

The older woman had stored all her hopes in that girl, and she couldn't forgive the younger woman for the disappointment she had brought in her heart.

Rebecca was just shoving her hands in Ariel's direction when Becka ran into the room. The young woman immediately understood what was going on and, narrowing her eyes to thin lines, spread her fingers toward Rebecca. A powerful swirl of wind enveloped the older woman, spinning her on the spot.

The old woman wailed in evident distress, and Becka lowered her fingers. Rebecca breathed hard and slashed the small woman with a gaze full of hatred.

Becka tilted her head and raised her brows. "I can see what turns through your mind, grandma," she said casually. "Keep in mind that you might be more experienced, but I am stronger," she warned the older woman.

"Sit there, Rebecca," Bryan pulled the woman to an armchair and showed her to take a seat. "Don't move. Don't move even a muscle," he ordered her. "I'll have Becka take care of you if you don't behave," he threatened her, and the harshness of his features made the woman keep her mouth shut. The man was dead serious.

Then Bryan headed to Ariel and Max. "How is he?" he asked Ariel, kneeling next to them.

The young woman raised her head, and the sadness in her eyes cut through the man's heart. He noticed unshed tears in her eyes and shook his head in disbelief.

"He's breathing," Ariel touched Bryan's hand, realizing that the man had assumed the worse. "I don't know what else to do," she whispered.

"Call Aunt Marjorie," Becka proposed. "And Maggie," she said quickly, remembering that her cousin's gift was healing. Maggie was good enough, even if she hadn't refined her talent, either.

Ariel nodded. "I think this would be a solution," she agreed with Becka.

Bryan kissed the woman on top of the head and left to make the calls. Becka continued surveying Rebecca with implacable determination.

You understand that you're never welcome in this house again," Becka told her in an icy tone of voice. "You won't see us, and you won't see our kids anymore. I don't want you near them ever again."

Rebecca tried to say something, but Becka tilted her head and raised her left brow, and the woman kept her mouth shut. She remained seated, seething in silence, her hands folded primly in her lap.

Ariel studied her with detachment. The old woman didn't look too bad for the wear. Her snow-white hair was ruffled, but she hadn't suffered any other upset.

The young woman shook her head, disheartened that there was no fairness in that situation. Then, she leaned over Max again. The man still breathed, and that helped to keep her hope alive.

CHAPTER TWENTY-FOUR

Marjorie and Maggie left everything aside and came to Becka's house in less than ten minutes. Bryan had been succinct on the phone, but the women understood that things were dire.

Before leaving the house, Marjorie also called her father. She asked Adam to come and collect his mother from her niece's house. The woman told him that he needed to do something with Rebecca as the woman had become more unhinged than before.

When the two women got into the living room, they couldn't believe their eyes. Besides Becka, who looked like a powerful goddess, everyone else showed signs of terrible wear.

New wrinkles had appeared on Rebecca's face, and her lips seemed to have become thinner. Rebecca sat in an armchair with her hands folded in her lap and a mutinous expression on her face. With a dark light in her eyes, she watched what happened around. Her rigid posture betrayed her dissatisfaction with the younger people's actions.

Bryan applied pressure with his right hand over his ribs, a sign that he had been hurt, and Marjorie didn't like the distant light in his eyes.

The man had lounged on the sofa and put a baby monitor on the coffee table before him. Bryan had insisted on leaving the children to play upstairs. He didn't want them to witness what was going on with the adults downstairs.

Ariel didn't show any color in her cheeks, and her pale pink lips twitched involuntarily. The young woman held Max's head in her lap and brushed her fingers through the man's dark mane, trying to soothe him, although he was unresponsive.

The man's state worried both Marjorie and Maggie the most. The only good thing was that he still breathed. Otherwise, he didn't seem to respond to any stimulus, and when they touched him, he felt feverish.

Mother and daughter looked at each other, and with a nod, they began to take off the man's pullover and shirt. Once they finished, both women laid their hands on his bare chest.

They closed their eyes simultaneously. With an expression of maximum concentration on their features, the women tilted their heads back, pressing the clammy skin with their fingers. The spots under their fingers began getting warmer, and a glowing light traced the shape of their hands.

After a couple of minutes, the man's breathing turned from shallow to more profound. The women's features showed strain and fatigue. Marjorie opened her eyes and asked Ariel to join them. Ariel looked at her with puzzlement in her eyes, but then she put her hands on Max's skin with hesitation.

"Come on, Ariel," Maggie burst into laughter. "Don't be a chicken. We need you, girl."

Ariel stuck out her tongue to her cousin, but then she hard-pressed her palm to the man's chest and focused only on healing him.

Max opened his eyes after a few seconds, and his gaze stopped on Ariel's face. The man breathed deeply, sighed, and then said with a shake of his head, "You know that now you must marry me. You might have a whacky family, but you're worth it," he pointed out in a weak voice.

With a peal of shaky laughter, Ariel shook her head. "How did you get to that conclusion?" she asked him in an amused tone of voice, relieved to see that the man had mended.

"You saved my life, so you have to marry me," the man explained his reasons in earnest. "There's no way around that," he added, watching Ariel with hawk eyes. "You have to watch over me forever," he pointed out.

"Marjorie and Maggie saved your life," Ariel corrected his misconception. "Don't you think you should marry one of them?" she tilted her head, and her lips twitched with amusement.

"Nah," Max replied with a shake of his head. "They helped, maybe, but without you, they wouldn't have brought me back from the brink. By the way, I saw the light," he joked, wiggling his brows. "Anyway, I choose to marry you," he reiterated his wish.

"He's right, you know," Marjorie stroked her niece's arm. "Without you, we wouldn't have succeeded. We needed what you had in your heart," she explained.

"But you still have to go to the hospital to get stitches for that thing," Maggie showed Max the wound in his arm.

"Oh, not again," the man scowled with exasperation. "Lately, I've been in the hospital so often that I could practically sell my house and move in there," Max complained.

"I'm sorry," Marjorie told him. "There are things we're not allowed to do. You need to go to the ER for that."

The man groaned but accepted the inevitable. Then, to forget about what waited for him once more, he turned to Ariel with hope in his gaze.

"You haven't answered me. So, will you marry me?" Max asked her again.

"Of course, I will," she laughed with tears in her eyes.

"Soon?" the man insisted.

"As soon you want," she nodded. "You can even choose the place," the young woman offered with generosity.

"We can do it in the hospital," Max proposed wishfully, and everyone looked at him as if he had lost his mind. "Don't look at me like that," his gaze swept over the people in the room. "We've spent more time in that damn hospital lately than anywhere else. It's like mandatory to tie the knot in there."

"I hope you're joking, young man," Adam, Rebecca's son, intervened. "My niece won't get married in a hospital. Choose another venue," the man ordered with so much authority that Max felt the need to salute. The older man even exhibited the bearing of a general.

"Of course, sir," Max rushed to agree with him. "We'll get married after I get out of the hospital and in my house. I have a good security system, you know," he added, looking from one to the other. "That witch won't pass over the front door," he promised to Ariel, pointing toward Rebecca, and the young woman laughed at his words.

CHAPTER TWENTY-FIVE

In March, Ariel became Max's wife. They recited their vows in his house in front of the French doors that opened to the garden. The weather turned milder, and the sun shone brightly over their ceremony.

The entire Winston family was present, except for Rebecca. Anyway, her absence brought joy to Jay's heart. He couldn't stand the sight of his great-grandmother anymore. The others didn't miss her either. Rebecca had become too destructive lately, and no one wished to see what the woman could do next.

The wedding didn't go smoothly, but that was expected. No one in the Winston family chose regular people to marry, and there was always something.

This time, the bride took her sweet time to get ready in one of the guest rooms, and she was late for the ceremony. Max waited patiently for about twenty minutes, even though he began checking his watch since he strode to where the pastor stood.

With a grimace, the man noted that the moment when he should have gotten married had come and gone. Still, he remained on the spot making small talk with the pastor and Bryan, his best man.

At the twenty-minute mark, Max lost his patience, though. He marched out of the living room with heavy steps and ran up the stairs to Ariel's door, turning a deaf ear to his best man's pleas to continue waiting patiently.

"Ariel, if you don't come out of this room in five seconds, I'll come in and carry you downstairs myself," he warned the woman in a grave tone of voice. "You made a promise to me, and you will keep it even if I died in the process," Max ended his speech in a furious shout.

Emilie, who was just arranging her daughter's veil, froze and looked at the door with fearful eyes. Her soon-to-be son-in-law's stature and appearance already intimidated her. The thunder in his voice prompted her heart to sink in her boots.

"Don't worry, mother," Becka stroked the woman's shoulder. "I'll take care of him. Anyway, hurry, Ariel. I don't know how long I can keep him downstairs."

Becka kept her promise. She persuaded Max to come with her downstairs, but first, she had to vow to him that his bride would come in less than a minute.

"Brides need to look good, Max," she explained to the man. "Any bride needs to see her groom gazing at her in wonderment when she walks up the aisle. To get that effect, it takes time. Sometimes, it takes more time than you'd like. However, you have to give her that time. You owe it to Ariel," she warned him.

Becka delivered Max to Bryan, and sotto voce, the woman ordered him to keep a better watch over his friend. Afterward, Becka, who also was the matron of honor, left to welcome the bride in the hallway that led to the living room.

The rumor about what had happened started to spread through the guests when Emilie came downstairs. Emilie sat next to her son, Alex, and told him what transpired upstairs. Her loud voice reached the people in the second row, and from there, it was just a matter of time until everyone at the wedding learned the story.

The ceremony started amid chuckles and giggles, but Max didn't care. He already got what he had wanted since he laid his eyes on Ariel the first time. And the man didn't even need to remember Becka's words when Ariel started down the makeshift aisle. His bride took his breath away.

The young woman looked like she had just stepped out of a fairy tale. Her diaphanous dress showed the perfect shape of her shoulders and the line of her waist. Her head held high, Ariel moseyed down the aisle with the bearing of a princess. The beaming smile on her lips competed only with the bright lights dancing in her gaze.

Max lost any coherent thought and stared at her with his lips parted and his hands fisted. The man summoned his strong will to control himself. He knew that he couldn't give in to his basic instincts. However, he wished he could have snatched his bride and locked himself with her in one of the rooms, as far as possible from the guests.

The pastor had to clear his voice a few times to attract the man's attention to him. He threw Max a reproachful gaze, but the young man just shrugged. In his opinion, if a man wasn't spellbound by his bride on his wedding day, then something was seriously wrong.

The pastor asked if anyone had anything to say against the union. Most of the Winston family's members turned to the door. Almost all of them expected to see a vengeful Rebecca, ready to spew curses against the bride and the groom. They had already witnessed that in the past, after all.

Max tilted his head toward Ariel and whispered, "Don't worry, Ariel. Rebecca can't get in here. The people at the gate have her general description. And after all, I don't see Rebecca jumping a fence. However, if she does, the alarm system will announce the guys I hired for the day. Anyway, it's funny how everybody is quaking in their boots that your great-grandma would interrupt our wedding."

The woman shook her head but didn't reply. She turned toward the pastor and waited for the ceremony to end so that she'd become Max's wife.

A stray sunray shone over the young woman's features, and the groom's breath hitched. His bride looked happy and serene.

At that moment, Max wished for a happy and peaceful marriage. Still, the man doubted he could have everything. The last few days had taught him that peace wasn't something that lasted long between his bride and him.

Anyway, his life was full of passion and lacked any hint of boredom. That had to be enough. Max was convinced that peace was vastly overrated, after all.

EXCERPT FROM
"DOUBLE-EDGED"

The young woman sat in a cushy armchair in the lobby, an open magazine on her lap. She pretended interest in a story she was reading.

She wore a wide blue slouch-hat, designed to cover half her face. It matched the short summer dress that showed off her long, tanned, and shapely legs.

A pair of big, black sunglasses completed the ensemble. She resembled Audrey Hepburn in the film Charade. Her eyes, hidden behind the black lenses, carefully watched the people that came to the front desk and talked to the receptionist.

She had already arranged with the much younger man at the front desk to signal her when the person she was interested in would come. He was supposed to raise his hand, as if he said, *just one moment, please.* Then, he would turn away for a couple of seconds and check something on the monitor.

Since her watch began, two couples had already passed by the front desk and talked to the clerk. They had just taken their keys and left immediately, so she didn't bother with them anymore.

Finally, after a few more minutes of impatient waiting, a tall, dark man came to the reception area and spoke to the clerk. The clerk nodded and raised his hand, the sign they had pre-arranged. He checked his computer screen for a couple of seconds, nodded again, and then took a bag from behind the counter and handed it to the man.

The man took the bag with a nod and turned around. His eyes brushed expertly over the people in the lobby. He left the impression he was mildly curious, yet he analyzed everyone carefully. She watched him furtively from her under lashes so that she wouldn't expose herself.

She imagined that her appearance didn't impress him. He looked her over, from head to toe, taking his time when he swept over her legs, but then he turned around and went toward the elevators. Probably, he didn't think that she posed any danger, so he didn't worry about her.

Once more, her senses didn't perceive anything clear about him. She realized she had stumbled onto the first person in the world that she couldn't read at all. That annoyed and frustrated the woman even more than before.

She had believed that she would be able to peek into his mind if she were in his presence. It made sense that she wouldn't encounter any barriers. She had been wrong. The man remained entirely obscure to her reading.

When he disappeared, she stood up with lazy and fluid movements. She laid the magazine on the table near the armchair. She had all the time in the world, so she smoothed her skirt with long and light strokes. Her eyes swept over the hotel lounge, furnished with taste and comfort in mind.

With lazy strides, she went to the front desk. The clerk beamed at her warmly. He hurried toward her as if the other client didn't matter at all.

She noticed his rush and considered that the big tip she had given him earlier determined his behavior. Yet, something else lay behind the young man's grin. He had enjoyed their game and even imagined all sorts of thrilling scenarios.

His age, as well as her appearance, had fueled his imagination. Her hat and big sunglasses, as well as the vague clandestine air of the entire affair she had involved him in, had made him feel like James Bond or someone similar.

"I think I'll be leaving this afternoon. I won't wait until morning. However, don't worry. I'll pay for the night," she said to the young man with an apologetic smile. She knew that he had been hoping for something more. He hadn't thought that the adventure would end there.

Yet, she had been interested in one scene only. That had already ended, although the result disappointed.

"We're very sorry you're leaving, ma'am. Didn't you like your suite?" the young man inquired, and worry wiped the smile off his lips.

"Oh, yes, I did. Don't worry about that," the woman reassured him with a wave of her hand and a bright smile. "But, you see, I've already rented a house on the beach for a few days. So, I thought to take advantage of it right now, you know," she beamed brightly at the clerk again. "I've got the sea and a pool just for me there... Would you mind preparing the bill before I get back downstairs with my luggage?"

"No, of course, not. Your bill will be ready, ma'am," the man promised and rushed to the computer to prepare it.

AUTHOR'S BIO

Rowena Dawn writes romance, reads thrillers and watches comedies. She likes walking through the woods but insanely loves the sea. She has a love-hate relationship with her writing and drives her dog crazy whenever she doesn't stop writing to take him out.

OTHER BOOKS BY ROWENA DAWN

Becka's Awakening – Book One in the Winstons series

Matt's Dilemma – Book Two in the Winstons Series

Jay's Salvation – Book Three in the Winstons Series

Ariel's Dream – Book Five in the Winstons Series (forthcoming)

Leap of Faith

Double-Edged – Book One in the Perfect Halves Series

Eyes in the Dark – Book Two in the Perfect Halves Series

Pulled In – Book Three in the Perfect Halves Series

Mr. (Almost) Right